SURRENDERED

BY

PEGGY PATRICK

ISBN-13: 978-0-9962959-0-1
ISBN-10: 0996295909

DEDICATION

SURRENDERED is for you...Lisa, my daughter...my friend...my editor...my laugh-a-minute. Thank you for all hours you spent working with me and for making this experience a blast! I love you.

ENDORSEMENTS

I would highly recommend this book it was a fantastic read!! Once I started reading it I couldn't put it down until I finished it! I can't wait to start on the next one and am even planning on giving the book to a few co-workers for a birthday or Christmas gift. I saw a few comments above regarding the sex it is VERY PG especially if you compare to what's on the TV now days. I would have no problem letting a teenager read this book. In my opinion it's explained in a beautiful & tasteful way and teaches morals!!!! I loved the book and I know you will to!!!!! *****Ashley Smith

I loved this book! It could easily be a made into a movie for Lifetime! A sweet love story. I could not put it down, I was cooking dinner reading this book! I cannot wait to read her next book! One of the other reviews said the sex part after they were married should be rated R, but I thought the author did a very tasteful job. The ending would not have been as sweet as it was without it, after all isn't sex a gift from God to be shared between a husband and wife?
*****Deana Corson

Very, very good...I am not a huge fiction reader; however, I really enjoyed this story line! I'm anxious to read the next book :) *****Dana Cook

This is an amazing book, storyline, characters and everything you expect in a book. The author set a beautiful scene and storyline right up front. I did not want to put the book (iPhone) down and it kept my attention on every page. I cannot wait till another book comes out by Peggy Patrick. She is an awesome writer. *****Page Sampley

This was an awesome book. I could not stop reading it. Anytime I had to put it down I could not wait to get back to it! I loved the whole idea. The story is SO real!!! *****Rose Dickerson

CHAPTER ONE

From the day the letter arrived, Toni hadn't once asked herself if she was doing the right thing. When she set her mind to something, only an act of God could stop her and so far nothing that big had shown up.

Toni knew she hadn't fully thought this thing through, but that wasn't totally unlike her. Uncle John had told her many times the day would come when her impulsive spirit would land her in an alligator pit.

So far, her only regret was saying goodbye to Julie Langston, the closest thing she could claim to family. Her best friend and roommate for the past three years had driven her to the Dallas airport this morning, told her for the hundredth time how senseless she was, cried and wished her luck because she would need a lot of it.

Toni Barton had always managed to walk through the hard places in her life with more than a fair amount of ease. This wasn't hard, but pure bliss.

But, Lord help her, this opportunity to live, work, eat and sleep her dream wasn't going to pass her up. If it did turn out to be a fiasco, she'd find that out when it happened.

Right now, she was on the last leg of her journey to a new job; a dream come true. She felt her heart pounding in anticipation of a glimpse of the ranch and getting on with the more earthy breed of life that had all but consumed her years ago.

She remembered well when her blood first started turning into horse grain, as Uncle John use to tell her. She'd been ten years old when her parents died together in a car crash. Her first month was spent in a foster home in Dallas until her mother's bachelor brother came and took her home.

Thus, she began a new life on Uncle John Baxter's ranch where she was given her first horse, a gentle, aged gelding she called Straw. She remembered Uncle John's loud belly laugh at her complaints about the animal's lack of energy. She remembered the afternoon she sneaked away into the open field on his own bay cutting horse to prove her capabilities. The horse proved more than she could handle until she was suddenly grasped around the waist and swung unceremoniously behind a rider on another horse, while her mount was ponied home. Before her feet were allowed to touch ground, praise for her know it all riding ability came with a swat on the seat of her pants from Cowboy and a mean command to sit on the corral fence where he could keep an eye on her until John returned from his errand.

Toni hadn't dared to tell her uncle about the incident, but guessed Cowboy had when John's wrinkled brown face lighted in a knowing smile at supper that evening and asked if she had any new saddle sores.

Cowboy, she never did know his real name, worked almost four more years for Uncle John before suddenly moving on. She smiled to herself now remembering the many times after Cowboy's departure that she had wished he was around to see her ride the young horses brought in to break. She told herself she just wanted to *show him*, but she had lain in the hay loft the day he left refusing to say good bye. She cried until her throat hurt when his pickup and horse trailer disappeared from view of her hide-out. At fourteen, she had suffered her first broken heart.

For the next five years, Toni spent every waking moment that she wasn't in school doing ranch chores and riding every horse she could persuade Uncle John to let her on. He'd told her once if she ever fell off and busted her head open, a whole bunch of little horses would pour out of her brain.

The horses had become a sanctuary of joy, a security of happiness in a child whose life of all that was familiar and safe had been torn from her in the space of one day. They were her first great and heroic love that rescued her after being cast out into a motherless world. These romantic and majestic friends had shown her the very heart of Almighty God, being specially created by Him just to make her smile. At least that was Uncle

John's brilliant answer when she'd asked him where horses came from. She chose to believe that long enough for the idea to draw her to this wonderful God who would do such a thing for her.

She swallowed and shifted on her seat willing away the sudden well in her eyes. In her mind's eye, she could see Uncle John just as she'd found him that morning when he didn't come to the kitchen for breakfast. She was told his heart just stopped.

Soon after, she learned the ranch would be put up for auction. John never talked about his debts and she decided it wasn't her business to know. Uncle John had provided her with the happiest years of her life, not to mention a fancier vehicle than he'd ever had for himself and a cell phone that she knew had been more for his peace of mind.

She decided to let Julie win one argument and leave her little red jeep in Texas for the time being. Driving to Wyoming alone didn't scare her, but she was anxious to get this show started and she could always fly back for a visit and drive it out then. Mostly, she just needed to get Julie out of her ear.

Uncle John had secretly squirreled away a good sized nest egg in Toni's name at the bank which she only learned about after his death. It paid for her college degree, giving her a career teaching high school language arts. She accomplished it in record time, knowing it was all for Uncle John more than for herself. He had preached at her constantly to *go to college, get that education, make something of yourself.* She hoped he somehow knew she had used his money well.

After the ranch was sold, she had hooked up with her high school pal and shared an apartment in Dallas up until this very morning. She chuckled out loud at the memory of Julie's hysterical, disbelieving face when she had shown her the personal resume she'd written to Mr. J.V. Luke to apply for a ranch hand job on the Double OO in Wyoming. Julie had done her best to dissuade Toni, but her own father had been the catalyst behind the fire that ignited in her to get back in the saddle.

It had started during a surprise visit one weekend from Dan Langston. He had brought a hand printed poster from his old buddy in Wyoming for experienced ranch help. It seemed to her he was deliberately trying to arouse her interest in the ad.

"Ain't got the stuff for it anymore, myself," he had laughed, "but thought of you, Toni when I read this. Ranchin' gets in the blood, I know for a fact it ain't easy to get rid of. And you always had a natural way with them green colts."

She had laughed with him, but her mind stirred up a serious scheme that she didn't doubt for one moment her ability to handle. But it was the yearning in her heart to return to the lifestyle she loved that spoke the loudest. For days afterward she thought of little else, especially with the *help wanted* ad taunting her from the kitchen table where it had been left.

The easiest thing she had ever done up to now was to resign from her teaching job. At least she had that career to fall back on if she needed it, but she had to follow her heart now. There was a compelling deep inside that took precedence over everything else, and she believed her Heavenly Father had swung open this door. Every time she entertained thoughts about making this drastic change in her life, and calling on God for His counsel, her heart rate literally kicked up a notch creating an unexplainable excitement inside of her. She knew. She just knew.

Toni sucked large breaths of the fertile Wyoming grass fields through the open back window of the cab. Julie had wished her luck before she left and the flight to Jackson had been uneventful, but she did find a piece of that luck on her side when she prepaid the taxi fare from the airport to the Double OO. Not on her life would she have divulged to Julie that she had made a financial decision she hoped she didn't regret. She had managed to pay out some outstanding bills left by her uncle, including a large part of his funeral expenses. Most of her teacher's salary was used each month to get that done and all but what she would need to make this *career* move finished paying off those debts. After paying the cab driver, she owned approximately seventy-five cents and all that three suitcases would hold.

Of course, she was far from destitute, but knowing she would be well set financially in only two and a half years didn't make her present pocket change look any better. Her parents had thankfully set up a trust fund for her early on and collectable on her twenty-fifth birthday. By then, she could buy her own ranch. She chose to see this spur of the minute move as prospecting for future investment.

She'd never been to Wyoming, but the scene that spread out before her was fiercely breathtaking. Summertime here was cool compared to Texas. The whole panoramic picture of the towering granite mountain peaks way off on the horizon, with miles of open grasslands leading to its base, had to be the Wind River Mountain Range. She knew the Double OO Ranch set just beneath those mountains.

Excitement exploded in her veins at first sighting of the ranch from the taxi cab as she absorbed the sight of the primitive cedar post fencing that ran all the way up the long drive from the cattle guard that set directly beneath the double crossbar entrance, then encircled the brown frame ranch house that gave a wide berth to other out buildings and livestock pens. The lawn and shrubs were thick with late spring growth and in dire need of attention. *Nothing fancy about this place.* But upscale wasn't a big attraction for her. It was the lifestyle, the animals, the sweet smell of grain and hay. Even cattle pen odors didn't offend her. She smiled remembering Julie holding her nose the few times she'd helped Toni do chores for Uncle John.

The sullen driver stopped immediately in front of the ranch house and without a word unloaded her bags from the car trunk and dropped them on the ground. She had just enough time to step out before the impudent driver sped away.

Flattering. She waited for the dust to settle around her, then stepped upon the small porch. She was amazed at the soft feel of the air around her. It seemed to wrap her like a sweet welcome hug. *Trust in the Lord and lean not to your own understanding.* Those words seemed to be part of the caressing breeze she felt.

Just as she raised a fist to knock, the heavy wooden door swung open by a graying, sun leathered man, cowboy from his tattered straw hat to his well rode boots and spurs. He looked as though she had just slapped him instead of knocked on the door.

She looked up at her fist, then back at the man. "Hi. I'm Toni."

"Ma'am," he acknowledged her, still staring until she wondered if she'd sprouted another head.

"You must be Mr. Luke.?" She stuck out her hand, hoping to snap him back from the jolt that her appearance seemed to have given him.

"No, ma'am. I work for him."

A smile lit her face, almost relieved. "Oh. Well, he's expecting me. About a job."

Fresh surprise flared in him. He still hadn't invited her inside.

"Well, I mean, he wasn't exactly expecting me *this* afternoon, but as soon as I could come."

The man's eyes softened finally as he stepped to the side, a sheepish smile deepening the age telling lines in his face. "Come in, hon. I'll go get him."

She stepped past him into the spacious room, swallowing past the memory of Uncle John that the old cowboy invoked. He exuded a quiet gentleness that was so much like her uncle. She missed him terribly right this minute.

The rays of a late day sun was streaming through the window, magnifying the dusty, cluttered ranch style furnishings set haphazardly round the den. She absently registered the fact that not much housekeeping was happening here, when the nicker of a colt drew her to the window on the back side of the room. A nostalgic shudder surged through her as motion in a riding arena caught her eye.

Two yearlings bucked and played like they'd just been turned out of their stalls to get some exercise. Her eye traveled past them to follow the endless stretch of flat grasslands that turned into a tree lined horizon. And beyond that, the mountains.

She stood mesmerized by the invigorating scene out the window, breathing in smells of horse and dust and real life, until the masculine drawl behind her reeled her back inside.

"I understand you're looking for work, Toni is it?"

She wheeled around to find one of the most roguishly attractive faces she'd ever seen. He was younger than she had expected. Her heart fluttered off beat and she prayed he couldn't see the heat that she could feel cooking her face. His gaze unapologetically moved up, then down her length, his stance declaring he was in charge here. Only a flicker of pleasure gleamed in his eyes as he, *all man like*, checked out her body proportions before it disappeared. But she saw. For an instant, she felt as if an invisible current bound the two of them together.

His hair was thick and smooth and as black as coal. There was something striking in his ice blue eyes, something almost familiar about him. She seemed to be caught in a spell, unable to look away, but aware of a tension mounting. He stood a good eight inches above her, holding his broad shouldered frame erect but relaxed. Somehow the man didn't fit in with the scenery in this house. He had a classy richness about him, directly contrasting the old fashioned furnishings and dirt they were standing in the middle of. His western dress shirt was bright white against sun browned skin, and unbuttoned a quarter ways down, revealing a silver chain nestled in a mat of black hair. The sleeves were rolled up just below his elbows. Brand new dark denim wranglers sported a gleaming silver belt buckle, the tiny row of diamonds inset in the letter L holding her stare too long. Besides the burn in her cheeks, she felt an unaccustomed quiver shoot through her middle.

"Toni Barton." She moved toward him extending her hand, feeling unsure of herself for the first time since she'd heard of the Double OO.

"Judd Luke." He clasped her small hand covering it entirely with long work roughened fingers, one of them sporting a silver horseshoe ring with tiny diamonds that sparkled around the U-shape of it in flashes of red and blue. The man was a mixture of hard work and diamonds, sun leathered bronze skin and an air of ritzy refinement. He released her quickly. "I apologize, Miss Barton. I had asked around for a housekeeper a while back, but I've changed my mind." He smiled politely dismissing the whole conversation, turned and strode toward the front door. "I apologize again for your inconvenience."

Mutiny seized her emotions momentarily before she blinked it to the background and calmly decided that her name had simply slipped his mind. After all, it had been a few weeks.

She smiled nervously. "I'm not exactly here looking for work. You've already hired me, about a month ago."

He studied her intently, then a slight annoyance darkened his already gruff, short-bearded features as he pulled open the door letting it bump against the wall. "If I had hired you, I would remember."

Defiance broke loose; her blood began to dance. She had gone to too great a length to get here to let that door hit her in the rear this fast. "I have written proof, Mr. Luke, signed by you that my employment would begin the day I arrived at this ranch."

"Written pr...." He rolled his eyes. "Doing what, exactly?"

"Anything the rest of your hands do around here." Her chin tilted confidently upward.

She watched the man lean back casually against the wall, light a cigarette and take a long drag. For several seconds he didn't speak and Toni curiously scrutinized those unusually blue, but caustic, angry eyes, watching as they set themselves into a serious crease. Then he spoke slowly.

"Ten seconds, Miss Barton, is all you have to produce your written evidence."

Her teeth clenched at his arrogance. If she had any sense, she'd walk out and forget she ever heard of the almighty Double OO, but seventy-five cents wouldn't get her to the cattle guard. Withdrawing the envelope from her purse, she walked stiffly across the room and laid it on his open palm.

She expected him to recognize it and then rip it up. Instead, he opened the letter and she watched the color in his face pale as he read in silence. He handed it back to her, then calmly closed the door.

"It seems we have an odd situation here," he said slowly and with less attitude.

"Are you saying that you did hire me?"

"No, I'm not saying that." He raked a hand through his silky black hair and even amid the angry confusion, she couldn't help but admire the handsome, almost familiar little-boy expression that crossed his face.

"That letter was written by my father," he said finally. "His initials were the same as mine."

Toni looked stricken as she caught the *were*.

"He died unexpectedly two weeks ago."

She closed her eyes a moment feeling desperate. "I'm so sorry," she said, her sympathy genuine.

His eyes moved with consideration over the layered light brown curls that fell in the direction of their choice, then studied her face, forming an insulting smirk on his lips.

"You have only yourself to blame for this, you know," he stated flatly.

She felt bewildered. She was realistic enough to know Judd Luke could not be held responsible for something his father had done. Anyway, he was right. Her common sense must have been out to lunch on this deal.

"So, he didn't tell you about me...about hiring me, I mean."

"No, but he's famous for that. Springing surprises was his favorite thing to do." He smiled to himself. "I'm sorry you had to be his last hoorah. We break colts here, but mainly run a few hundred head of beef cattle. That's out of your job description, I'm sure. If I were you, I'd find out what I was getting myself into before..."

"Never mind," she interrupted his scolding. "Here, I'm sure you have a file thirteen around here somewhere." She pushed the envelope and its contents into his hand, then let herself out the front door. Her eyes misted with regretful tears, her main regret that she only had access to a few coins and three bags of personal belongings. But her adrenaline was flowing angrily giving her enough stamina to hoist the smallest case under one arm, grasp the other two in each hand and walk briskly down the long drive.

Only after reaching the entrance gate did she allow her taut nerves to slacken. She believed she would have sat down and cried a while if she hadn't caught sight of a horse and rider standing across the pasture, staring in her direction. Instead, she swallowed the lump and carefully walked the rails of the cattle guard, sympathizing with dudes who had been forced to walk the plank of a ship. Just when a wonderful dream was at her fingertips, reality showed up and slapped her hands. Only this time, reality was for her an unambiguous nightmare. If she managed to get back to Dallas, her only hope was Julie. But the thought of going backward was disheartening, to say the least. She had gone as far backwards as she cared to, having already discovered there was no cell phone service in this area.

A quick glance back showed her she was well out of sight of the Double OO. She heaved a sigh and staggered off the road's edge a few feet before dropping her load. Her arms throbbed from the constant stretching and she sunk onto the grass exhausted. Maybe for the first time in her life, she had become fully aware of lonely. She'd never particularly had a problem with fear, and still wasn't afraid. Just so terribly alone. She shook her head, refusing the welling tears that stung her eyelids.

By all indications, she had missed God by several hundred miles, and picked up a scolding from an egotistical bigot for her trouble. *Leaning on her own understanding* would not be a problem. She had none.

Before she could form a constructive thought, a motor hummed in the distance. Shading her eyes, she saw the front-end outline of a pickup. With fresh life suddenly pulsing through her limbs, she jumped up and waved her arms. At least she might get the fifteen miles to town. She ran toward the truck as the driver, wearing a cowboy hat, pulled over and turned off the engine.

"Hello," she called out and approached the open window. "I could use a lift to..." her voice fell silent as she stopped a few feet from the vehicle and found herself looking into the angry eyes of Judd Luke. Lord, he needed to lighten up!

Before she could loose herself from the shock, he shoved open his door and reached her in two strides. He clutched a handful of her hair and more gently than he looked, pulled, forcing her face straight upward. Her startled shriek went unheeded as he studied her face with a strange concentration.

"It's you!" he exclaimed wide-eyed. "Well, I'll be...And you haven't managed to grow up yet!"

"Well, it's only been an hour!" she stormed at him, jerking backward when his grip loosened. Had the man lost his marbles? She rubbed the back of her head.

"What are you doing walking this road? You could have told me you were on foot."

"Oh and you would have been happy to help me out."

"At the least, you could have called a cab."

"On seventy-five cents!" She hadn't meant to blurt out that revelation, but he didn't seem moved by it.

"I can cash a check for you, but I can't read your mind. Get in." He picked up her suitcases and placed them carefully in the back. That was the first gentle thing she'd seen out of him.

Reluctant and relieved she climbed in, wondering how she would get past the fact that she had closed her bank account before she left Dallas. Uncle John had drilled into her head to never, never, never use a credit card. Pay cash as you go. This was the first time she wished she hadn't learned his old fashioned ways so well, even if he hadn't fully abided by his own advice. It was probably his accrued debts that she'd paid on so faithfully the past few years that kept that advice ringing in her ears. It wasn't until they were back at the ranch when she had to state the amount she'd need that she told him the truth.

Dagger sharp blue fire stared her down from behind the elaborately handsome cedar log desk in his office. Disgrace was a new emotion for her, but it was against the Baxter blood in her to crumple at a bump in the road. She tilted her chin, refusing to give in to the humiliation he demanded.

He leaned back in the brown leather winged desk chair, head tilted back like a statue full of itself, a twisted smile on his face.

"People learn by their mistakes, Toni Barton, but there's an exception to every rule." His eyes flickered down the length of her, then back to settle on the confused squint in her eyes. "You've grown into an attractive woman. But that high and mighty do-it-yourself attitude is still getting you into trouble, I see."

Now it was her turn to stare like a cow at a new gate. "I'm sorry. Did I miss something?"

"Suppose you give Uncle John a call and let him know you're in a bind. If my memory serves me right, you're the very apple of his eye."

A mild wave of shock gripped her, holding her in silent place. Judd Luke knew Uncle John? Knew her? Something began to stir inside her mind and strangely in her heart. She found herself unable to take her eyes off of the man sitting before her and again sensed a familiarity in those eyes, compelling blue eyes that could draw a fourteen year old girl into her first crush.

"Cowboy?" She forced the whisper from her throat. "Cowboy," she repeated a little louder. The strange joy that leaped into her heart quickly dissipated with the glittering fire in his eyes that bored into her.

"Dear Uncle John never could bring himself to discipline you. And what a foolish little creature you've turned out to be, traipsing off across country without a whole dollar." He pushed a telephone across his desk in front of her demanding, "Call Baxter and tell him where you are."

Toni's mouth fell open. She was stunned and angry and unable to find the right words just then to put this ogre in his place.

"Did you hear what I said?"

"I heard you." She finally hissed, glaring down at his stone stiff face. She felt like she was riding a shock wave, stunned to see him after all these years. He had changed. He was taller, still bronc rider slim, but his chest and shoulders were broad, full. And his face. She could see him so clearly now. The years had been more than kind. Even the short black stubble beard fit his well-defined face. The young cowboy from her past was no longer that. She was having a stare down with the man he had become.

Her pounding heart gave her voice a kick start. "Uncle John died three years ago."

His eyes widened with surprise, his expression losing the stiffness, but Toni couldn't feel any triumph at turning the tables somewhat.

"I didn't know."

"There's a lot you don't know, but that doesn't matter. I've been on my own since then and managed just fine until...this job fell through." Her voice shook with indignation.

"In other words, this is all my fault."

"I didn't say that."

He couldn't help noticing how fragile she looked. She wasn't much taller than he remembered her as a fourteen year old, but her slender curves could not be proportioned more perfectly. "And suppose I pay your way back to Dallas. What's waiting for you? A home? Your teaching position?"

Her head jerked back in surprise. "How did you know I...?"

That was quite an impressive application you sent my dad, for a petite young woman who looks like she's spent all of her life inside the house."

She ignored the cynicism. It didn't matter whether he believed her qualifications or not. Her state of employment here was no longer the issue.

"I have a home...and...a...job." She felt her face warm at this small stretching of the truth and figured on getting her just reward for it sooner or later.

However she hadn't expected it *this sooner*. Within a couple of seconds, Judd was around the desk, caught hold of her shoulders and gave her a slight shake.

"How about some truth?"

Judd had whipped her senses into an outrage, but the fact that he seemed to know as much about her as she did stilled her tongue.

"How did...you know that I...?"

"That you're a liar?" Judd finished for her. "Phone numbers on your application. One simple call and I know you have no place to rush off to."

A roll of dejection edged down her spine. She'd never been called a liar and hated the sound of it. Everything inside of her went very still. She lowered her eyes and stared silently at the round toes of his boots that stuck out from under the scrunched bottoms of his jeans. She was not a liar. And he was not a flirty kid learning to be a cowboy. He was a man, a stranger, who was making the middle of her belly grab with strange sensations. She shouldn't give a real flip what he thought of her. But she did.

Without looking up, she offered, "I'm sorry I lied to you." And she truly was.

"Well don't expect that humble little apology to get you a..."

"I don't expect anything from you," she interrupted, as her eyes jerked back to his. "I am simply sorry I lied. What more do you want from me?"

He looked hard at her, a thoughtful squint creasing the corners of his eyes. Finally he spoke with a dead-level calm. "Beginning tomorrow morning, I want a solid eight hours work a day, six days a week until you've earned enough to leave here properly with."

Shock hit her first, then a renewed hope softened her expression. "You mean the job is mine?"

"*A* job," he corrected her. "You can work here as a housekeeper. I'll pay you minimum wage."

Her expecting expression fell to her ankles. Her immediate urge was to refuse. The glitter in his eyes said he had her and knew it, but there was little she could do in her present state of no place to go and no money to get there.

"Thanks for the favor, Cowboy." She couldn't hide the sarcasm.

His gaze didn't waver. "The favor is for John Baxter. He was a good man. You are a responsibility, nothing more. You'll earn every dime you get and when you leave here, my hands will be washed of any trouble you bargain for after that. Have I made myself clear?"

Toni couldn't see a hint of the laughing, mischievous Cowboy she had cried over so many years ago. This man was someone else, angry and bitter. She had no idea what she had gotten herself into. The joy of running out to meet her dream head on had turned, without warning, into a pile of poop. At least her boots were high tops.

She nodded her head. "Perfectly clear."

***

CHAPTER TWO

"Am I to assume I'll be sharing this house with you...alone?"

His laughter, mixed with mockery in those sapphire eyes, made Toni's cheeks flame. "You would be willing to work side by side every day with a ranch full of virile, red blooded men without concerning yourself with what trouble you might land in and you're worried about that? Just where had you planned on spreading your bedroll as a ranch hand?"

She stared at him, then shuffled uncomfortably as she looked away from his measuring glare. "I hadn't thought about that."

0   How old are you now, twenty something?"

"Twenty-three."

"There's been a man in your life somewhere, I'm sure, and you expect me to believe you didn't think about the fact that you would be entering a man's world out here?"

His accusations were obscene and unwarranted. But it would be a waste of time to argue the point. His mind was made up. Her whole heart, body and bloodstream were sold out to ranch life, second only to God Himself.

As for a man in her life, there hadn't been time for more than a few casual dinner dates, and no one who was particularly memorable. But that, she concluded was none of his business and swallowed the defensive swell in her throat.

She watched as he calmly lit a cigarette, then perched himself on the edge of his large pine desk

"You should know that you'll be the only woman on this entire ranch." He stood abruptly, moved around behind his desk and smashed his cigarette out in the ashtray. His palms rested on the glass top as he leaned forward slightly, a scowl darkening his face. "And I'll tell you this only once. I will *not* tolerate you messing around with my men. Your job description entails all housekeeping duties and I expect you to stay out of sight of my stockmen."

Toni's eyes flashed, but she managed, with effort, to swallow the blast of words shooting through her mind. "You've made your point," she said stiffly, "and I assure you, I have every intention of keeping my nose to the grind if it will get me out of here sooner. Now if you're reasonably satisfied, you can show me to the *maid* quarters."

She watched him straighten. He motioned her to follow, then disappeared into the hallway.

From what she had seen of the rest of the house, she wasn't surprised to find the guest room a disaster, too. The ash tray was full and a strong stifling odor of stale cigarettes lingered in the air. Dirty coffee cups were everywhere. Without another word, the big brawny cowboy left her to figure things out for herself.

Angrily, she swiped at a tear that had been wanting to escape for most of the day, a day she knew she would not have to enter into a journal in order to remember every detail of it. The only hope she had of escaping her iniquitous captor was Julie. She would get money for her somehow, but Toni couldn't bring herself to imposition her best friend. She had stepped off into this by herself. She would see it through the same way.

Willing a fresh batch of grit into herself, she got up and stripped the rumpled sheets off the bed. The utility closet in the hallway actually had clean sheets in it. After remaking the bed, she collected two hands full of dirty cups to haul to the kitchen.

"You don't go on payroll until morning."

She wheeled around too fast at the voice behind her, and tipped the stacked dishes off balance. Quick as lightning, Judd was in front of her with large outstretched hands halting the fragile avalanche.

Toni blinked feeling helplessly dismayed at her clumsiness. Then for the split moment that motion was silenced, their eyes met only inches apart. The odd, disturbing look he gave her was brief, but something in it caused tiny tremors to shoot up and down her spine. Flushing slightly, she ignored it and considered instead what he'd said.

"I'm aware of our arrangement, Mr. Luke, but I do have to sleep in here." Putting a formal edge on his name seemed to reduce the unnerving paroxysm inside her.

His blue eyes registered a cool dryness. "I'll help you carry these to the kitchen, but save the dish washing until tomorrow." He took one handful from her and stalked out. She shrugged and followed, carefully setting her load in the sink beside his.

"You'll find sandwich stuff in the refrigerator. Make yourself something to eat. You'll need the strength tomorrow," he stated matter of fact before disappearing into the adjoining laundry room and out the back door into the near darkness.

You can say that again, she thought, flicking a disheartened gaze over the kitchen. "Actually, a bulldozer could do this place a favor," she mumbled as she slapped a plate of ham on the small round maple dining table.

Judd stood outside the backdoor and sucked some badly needed fresh air into his lungs. He cursed as he raked his fingers through his hair, then dropped his arms heavily to his sides. "What on God's green earth were you thinking, Dad?" He whispered in exasperation. The exasperation was due to the twisted knot in his gut and the tight ache in his chest at the little heartthrob from his boyhood years, turned the woman and suddenly living in his house. And a gorgeous woman, at that. What in blazes was *he* thinking by letting her stay?

Later, Toni lay across the turned down covers on her bed. She had practically inhaled the sandwich and a hot shower had relaxed her tight muscles. The coolness of the moonlight created a hazy glow across her darkened room, while her thoughts ran rampant. The mental picture of Cowboy, as she used to know him, tall, but bone thin and always taking time to playfully yank her pigtails and laugh at her put-on agitation, was such a contrast to the big brawny man with black face stubble and features leathered by seasons of wind and sun and a way nasty attitude about females. He used to tease her, promising to marry her if she'd run an errand for him. She couldn't restrain the smile that played at her lips remembering how she had actually taken his charm straight to heart and how badly he'd broken that same heart when he left.

She raised up and scooted beneath the covers, annoyed at the strange disturbance in her heart. She reminded herself that it was natural for a girl to feel some form of pain when her life was so suddenly scrambled with uncertainty.

She closed her eyes for a few moments and when she opened them, the moonlight had been replaced by loud rays of sun. She got up and dressed hurriedly. The thought of a reprimand from the boss on her first day of work didn't thrill her a bit, but she was surprised that the house was as silent now as it had been when she went to bed last night. Great, she was alone.

She had expected to be responsible for preparing the lord and master's meals, but had that been true, she was sure she would have been bodily rolled out of bed.

After swallowing a slice of toast and cup of instant coffee, she opened the window over the sink and relished a few breaths of the cool morning air while preparing dish water.

It took several trips through the house to gather the scattered dirty dishes. Three hours later, she stood back to examine her arduous labor. The spacious ranch styled kitchen had actually been transformed right under her own hands. Underneath the dirt and clutter, she discovered a very warm, comfortable atmosphere and couldn't help feeling proud of herself.

The red brick-look linoleum was all she lacked in that room and after she swept the loose dirt away, she realized she'd saved the worst till last. Unable to find a mop, she rolled up her sleeves and sunk to the floor Cinderella style, scrubbing inch by inch until the hot sudsy bleach water burned her raw palms.

Something caused her to half turn her head and then she realized she wasn't alone. Startled, Toni jerked up straight, whipping around until she found herself kneeling at Judd's feet, staring up at his intimidating bulk, her mouth lipped open. The sunlight streaming through the uncovered window gave his heavy skinned features a hard, ruthless look that aroused in unison, fear and an odd fascination.

He grinned from the side of his mouth, shaking his head. "I don't believe what I'm seeing."

0   She considered throwing the dirty towel into his arrogant face. "Well, what did you expect to find me doing?" Then on impulse, remembering the way he'd bashed her character the day before, she added sarcastically, "Or maybe I should ask, *who!*"

The impulsive wisecrack hit its mark, but not before the effect was more than she bargained for. His face turned as hard as granite, his hands like steel traps as he reached for her wrists and brought her to her feet.

"Just exactly what is that supposed to mean," he growled through a tight thinned mouth.

She didn't try to hide her contempt as she opened her eyes wide and tilted her head back for him to see. "You're the one who wants to think I'm so hot to trot for a man."

"You're a woman, aren't you? His hard face darkened and for only an instant she thought his eyes were seeing someone other than herself. Then he suddenly released her and walked out.

Not until she heard the door slam could she relax her stiff limbs. She felt ill, the comprehension of just how frightened she was of this stranger becoming a reality when she couldn't stop her legs from melting her back into place on the floor. With the back of her hand she swiped at the tears spilling onto her hot cheeks. *Lord, if You were going to make a mistake, did you have to start with me?* An answer to that self-doubting banter instantly breezed quietly through her mind. FEAR IS NOT OF ME. She straightened her back and sat still, wondering at the sweet warmth wafting through her entire body. Again, she could sense so intently that God himself had put her in the middle of this nasty floor for some reason. She forced herself back to her task and it was well after lunch before she stood back to view the fruit of her labor.

Despite the circumstances, she felt a sense of satisfaction in the work she'd done, but shook her head in disgust at her minds' image of a pleasant smile of appreciation on Judd

Luke's face. She wanted nothing from that man except a paycheck in due time. Never had she met a single human being who could infuriate her so much.

She turned and headed toward her bedroom to rest, unable to extinguish the strange tension throbbing in her veins and the taunting picture of a big shadow-faced cowboy who was looking at her, but seeing someone else entirely.

Toni awoke with a start. She glanced at the digital alarm clock and drew a deep breath as she read, four-thirty. Good, she thought after listening to the still silence in the house. Make haste with a few more chores and none would be the wiser. She gave her brown curls a quick flick with her fingers, then stopped a moment to examine her general appearance in the dresser mirror. She started to laugh at the black smudges that streaked across her forehead and down both sides of her face, but the sound froze in her throat as brown eyes met blue ones behind her through the mirror. A menacing satisfaction was smeared across his face. She turned and shot a slanted look in his direction.

"Well, now that you're thoroughly rested, suppose you take a walk outside with me."

She made no reply at first, but blinked in puzzlement trying to figure out the catch. Even though she sensed an aura of tension around him, his eyes were gently honest in his offer.

"That's very kind of you." She didn't try to suppress the sarcasm in her tone. The past couple of days had all but destroyed her Double OO appetite.

"Okay, look, Toni. I'm sorry. I had no right to put my hands on you the way I did."

His apology was unexpectedly sincere and she straightened her spine, suddenly feeling a pressure release. "Apology accepted. Should I assume that also goes for your verbal attack?" She was hoping to clear the air between them, but immediately saw that wasn't happening.

"If it makes you feel better."

"If that's how you feel, maybe you should rethink this little walk. Someone might *see* you, and far be it from me to darken your reputation." She turned away from him, but the approaching thud of his boots caused her to tremble ridiculously.

Gentle, but firm fingers pinched her shoulders forcing her around to see gravely set blue eyes looking deeply into her own. "You've given me no reason to think of you otherwise. No decent thinking woman would lay herself open to the seduction of a ranch full of strange men. And you certainly had no qualms about taking up residence with me."

"You left me no choice, if you'll remember," she bit back. She knew it would be a waste of time to argue the other point. He had already chosen to believe the worst of her.

"*You* left *yourself* no choice when you came here in the manner you did." His regard remained steady but her pulses ran amuck when a big calloused hand reached to press itself against the side of her neck. A thumb under her chin tilted her head back. She shivered under the cool study of his stare that seemed to probe right through to her bone marrow.

"Toni?"

Alarm widened her eyes at his deliberately sensuous tone and with the nearness of him combined, she thought he was going to kiss her. She didn't move. An unseen force seemed to hold her still. Her heart began pounding crazily. Would she allow his lips to touch hers? Why did he even want to the way he felt about her? Her mind spun like a whirlwind. His mouth parted and she stiffened, then...

"Go wash your face," he grinned, with a sprightly gleam in his eyes.

She struggled inwardly with herself for several seconds. He had baited her and she had reached for it. She jerked away from his touch and that devastating triumphant grin.

"The grand tour starts in fifteen minutes. Be ready." He turned and left.

Strangely she felt easier that he had reverted back to his commanding rudeness. She was more sure of him that way and more sure of herself.

Toni pulled herself together, showered and found Judd waiting in the den twenty minutes later.

He glanced at his watch, then openly ran his eyes down the length of her and back up. "Not bad," was his only remark and she wasn't sure if her timing or boots, jeans and loosely handing T-shirt was *not bad*. But either way, she wasn't out to win any points with Judd Luke.

She silently followed him outside and around to the side of the house, uncertain of his reason for this tour, but the familiarity of the life style stretched out before her appealed so strongly to her nature that she was lost in her own inner excitement.

The Double OO sprawled across the land as far as Toni could see in barns and outbuildings of various sizes and cedar rail fencing that crisscrossed like grass runners. Some intersected with others to form small pasture areas and pens. She gazed out across the fields, rich and green with new spring grasses, a red evening sun smoothing a day's end glow on the cheerfully colored wild flowers.

Her thoughts suddenly projected an image of a young teenage girl racing across the open fields on horseback, pigtails whipping her back in the wind, opening her memories of Uncle John and of the best years of her life.

She had always prided herself that she and her Uncle were not only like father and daughter, but best buds. He had openly reveled in her devotion, giving her every opportunity to live well loved, and seemed way proud of the fact that she grew into a horse lover like himself.

But he was more than a horse *lover*. He would have been better titled a Whisperer. She visualized him now entering a pen with a scared, often times abused horse. A young one or aged, he worked a soothing soft voiced magic that instantly began to heal their wounded souls. Murmuring close enough to the flighty animal's ear where only the man and the horse were privileged to know what was said, the fury and the fight mellowed quickly and Uncle John led the willing, teachable horse to the next stage of training.

John Baxter was a private man. He shied from public accolades and made light of his extraordinary gift, taking the secret into Heaven with him. Except for Toni.

When she was sixteen, he had requested one morning at breakfast that she follow him to the barn where a new older and extremely ill-tempered stallion had been brought in the night before. She had always respected his privacy in this matter and was shocked, but thrilled to her toes at the invitation.

She learned about the gift that morning and discovered she did indeed possess it, as Uncle John had told her. And it was that very day that something took root deep inside of her spirit, a visceral something that skipped past her intellect.

At that remembrance, her lips pulled into a half smile, wondering if that was the same day her blood turned to grain.

It wasn't until Judd's deep voice pierced the air above her head that she returned. A quick glance at him told her he'd been speaking and was waiting for an answer.

"I'm sorry. What did you say?" She blinked quickly.

"Where were you, for heaven's sake?" He considered her questioningly as he held out a pack of cigarettes. "I asked if you smoked."

"No, I don't." She was beginning to wonder at his changing attitude toward her.

He didn't look at her then, but strode off toward one of the small outbuildings. She followed his long easy strides with short quick steps. Judd's sudden turnaround churned suspicions in her mind, but not enough to quell her eagerness for this grand tour.

The tantalizing scent of the hay barn drew her into a childlike delightful interest in his explanations of what each building and fenced pen were used for. She was amazed at the sizable operation he was running, definitely a contrast to Uncle John's smaller version. Resting her arms on a gate rail, she became fascinated watching the new baby colts in the small pasture attack their mothers almost viciously for their supper.

But she was not so totally engrossed in the scenes of motherhood that she didn't sense a pair of cool blue eyes studying her intently. She couldn't deny there was still a certain magnetism about this Cowboy. He had drawn her when she was barely old enough to consider the appeal of the opposite sex. She fought now to relax against the turbulence stirring inside her, one she understood more clearly now, but refused to accept as more than a normal tendency between male and female.

-336   She tilted her head back slightly to accept the caressing breeze on her face, to focus her attention on the beauty of the countryside and away from the unnerving awareness of the man beside her. He was still staring at her and apprehensively she reached up to push a wild strand of hair from her face.

His hand came up in unison and so gently covered her wrist, drawing her hand out, palm upward, studying it strangely. She looked at him then, assuming a blank expression to hide her scattered composure. "I've never believed in palm reading, myself."

He smiled. "Suppose I give it a try. Maybe I can make a believer out of you."

"Thanks, but you couldn't possibly tell me a thing that I don't already know." She twisted her hand but he held tight.

"I'm sure you're right about that." There was a glint in his eyes. "I could have kissed you back at the house. Why do I have the impression you were disappointed when I didn't?"

"You're out of your mind." She made a stronger bid for freedom only to be stilled by an iron bar grip around her back.

"Maybe. But I'm not blind. However, I *was* just about to decide I'd been a little hasty in my calculations about you. You seemed to have a real interest in our little tour. Your eyes were all lit up at the sight of my babies out there." He tipped his head toward the mares and new foals in the pasture. His voice suddenly changed to a low, softer tone. "But then that could have been just a bid for a second chance at that kiss."

He slowly loosened the grip on her wrist and moved his other hand up to lay his palm against the side of her face with a feather light touch. She froze beneath the unexpected gentleness, but tilted her face up to meet his wide-open gaze. For the first time, she glimpsed the Cowboy she had fallen in love with so long ago. The kindness, playfulness, youthfulness looking down at her seemed frozen in time. Neither could move a muscle. Neither wanted to.

For what seemed like a long time, they stood still. She drank from a memory that seemed to be exploding right into her present. He allowed himself the freedom of feeling a desire that had lain dormant for too long, a desire to touch and to be touched.

It seemed the most natural thing in the world when he lowered his head and touched his lips to hers, soft, gentle, testing, until she pushed to deepen the pressure. Then all at once he abandoned the gentleness that he'd reined her in with and pulled her forcefully into him with both arms wrapped around her. He kissed her with a firm coercion, a building urgency that said the world would end if he stopped.

She felt his work calloused hand slide up under her T-shirt and rub the smooth bare skin of her back. Alarmed at the intense awakening in her body and the unaccustomed demands it was making on her, she pulled back and pushed against him. He released his hold and stepped back from her.

Trembling, she looked up to find him struggling to cover the desire swimming in his eyes with a sardonic smirk that finally won out.

"Well now, I suppose you're going to call this circumstantial evidence." A cynical smile twisted his rugged features.

"I didn't ask for that." Her voice trembled.

"Yes, you did. And enjoyed it too."

Judd's eyes suddenly darkened and seemed to intrude for an instant on another place and time and Toni remembered seeing that same blank anger earlier during their encounter in the kitchen. Who was she the whipping post for? Maybe another woman who had hurt him terribly? She felt her own anger mellow at this assumption. She wondered even more what was beneath the hardened surface of this man.

Peggy Patrick

Then he was looking at her again and the cold contempt she saw hurt.

"Cowboy...," she began uncertain, not really sure what she wanted to say.

"What is it?"

She stiffened at his biting tone. "I think I'll turn in." She said quickly, deciding to let sleeping dogs lie for now.

"What were you going to say, Toni?" He pushed.

"I...told you. I..."

"Something's on your mind."

Her thoughts were in chaos trying to decide how to approach such a private subject. Her heart hammered ridiculously. "It's, well, it's just that I feel you're taking something out on me that maybe belongs to someone else." She looked up and searched his face for a reaction, but his expression didn't change. "I'm not the one you're angry with, am I," the question came as a statement. She expected his anger to flare, but his face surprisingly took on a softer expression.

For a moment, he steadied her gaze with a composed amazement in his crystal clear eyes. "Goodnight, Toni," he finally said softly, then walked away into the evening dusk.

She walked slowly back to the house giving the cool night air the opportunity to soothe her tangled emotions. She hadn't expected her first day on the job to end with her heart wrung and feeling like a beating lump in her throat. She thought God could have prepared her just a little bit for such a drastic turn in her daily life, *before* chunking her out into the middle of it. But then she knew well that God's ways are not our ways and sometimes very hard to understand. But it would have been nice just the same.

A strange sense of loneliness engulfed her suddenly. She felt vulnerable and needy and she hated that. Cowboy's kiss. That's what it was. Something sweet and frightening and very private had opened up on the inside of her. She realized with a start that she wanted to feel his arms around her again. His kiss again. She had never felt this kind of desire for a man before.

Sleep was a long time coming that night.

***

CHAPTER THREE

Toni began her second day at the crack of dawn, stopping for a breather about midmorning. She hoped the endless workload would banish the restlessness sleep had failed to relieve, but her mind refused to leave the past twenty-four hours alone. And she thought, not so much about the shadows surrounding Judd Luke, but of the immediate change in herself.

Only a few hours ago, she would have given her right leg for a way off of the Double OO ranch. At this moment, however, she strongly desired a decent hint of approval from the ranch boss. This realization brought a disturbing quiver to her pulses and a heartfelt distress, but she had always had a knack for disregarding what she couldn't understand and clearing her head with a hard shake, she called upon that protective ability.

By three o'clock, she stretched her aching limbs deciding enough was enough. She made herself a cup of coffee and sat beside the den window where she noticed a half dozen men hanging over a corral fence. She wondered momentarily if Judd was among them but the scene of activity in the small arena took her attention over. A man wearing a blue denim shirt was attempting to mount a fidgety colt. The brim of his yellow straw was pulled low in front to shade his face.

Toni stood up and squinted at the glass pane for a better look, but the audience of cowboys blocked a good view. Judd's warning to stay out of sight of the hands crossed her mind, but the excitement got the best of her. She quickly plopped her cup into the kitchen sink and raced outside to watch. After all, she was a hired hand too.

She stopped a few yards away from the action where she had a clear view of the bronc rider. It was Judd. But the dust hadn't settled under her own feet before a young cowboy spotted her and nudged the man beside him. Suddenly she found herself facing a lineup of grinning, hat-tipping men. Moving her eyes away from them, her stomach muscles tightened, not from the flirty attention of the cowboys, but from the spitfire anger stabbing at her from inside the arena. Judd had dismounted and released the frightened animal to another man in the pen. Even with several yards and an iron rail fence separating them, she clearly saw ice-hard slits for eyes spelling danger for her. She was suddenly a little frightened.

She watched the men open a pathway between them as Judd climbed the high rails to swing himself over in one leap and stride toward her.

God how she wished she could twitch her nose and zap a few miles between her small body and this formidable muscle. But she couldn't and too quickly he had a solid grip on her wrist, squeezing until she gasped.

Judd's jaw muscles worked as he clenched and unclenched his teeth. He fought to downplay his anger in front of their grinning audience. "If you want to keep your health, don't contradict me." He pulled her into step beside him and forced her towards the ceasing whispers of the men.

"Gentlemen," his tone was suddenly calm and somewhat light, "I'd like you to meet Toni...my wife."

0 A painful squeeze on her wrist shut down the gasp that rose in her throat. Somehow she managed to smile through the handshakes and his congratulatory back slaps, wondering why the earth didn't open and slurp him right up.

Finally, Judd released her wrist and excused them both. A hand on her back pushed her the full yardage to the house and once inside, hard fingers caught her upper arm and pulled her like an unruly child into his private study.

"What did you think you were doing?" He shoved her away from him then clamped his hand to his hips as though to keep them under control.

"I'm the one who should be asking you that!" she retorted, trying to stay on top of the fear creeping up her spine.

"Not by a long shot! I gave you strict orders to stay out of sight when my men were working in the corral, didn't I?"

Toni swallowed. "I just wanted to watch the..."

"Didn't I?" he repeated, barely restraining his fury.

"Yes, but..."

"But what!"

"You...you didn't have to tell them I was your wife." She willed herself calm in an attempt to defuse his rage somewhat.

"Let me tell you something. I demand certain moral standards from my men when they are on this property. It's a rule I stress to every one of them the day they hire on. So far, I've had no trouble. What kind of respect do you think I'll get if they get the idea I've got a shack-up job going on here?"

She stared at him wide-eyed and expelled an exasperated sigh. "Well, what's done is done. Where do you suggest we go from here?" she asked, knowing full well she had just bought herself the boot...or a divorce. She fought to suppress the ill-timed laugh that was bubbling up inside of her.

He looked at her with a cool smirk. "Where else, my little wife?"

"What!" Her posture straightened.

"The reputation of this ranch is at stake, not to mention mine."

The laughter found its way out this time. Hysteria invaded her blood veins and it took great effort to speak without giggling. "You want...me to marry you...to save you...your..." she laughed without restraint then until a hand reached out to grip the curve of her waist and pull her breathless body against his. Without preliminaries his free hand tangled itself in her hair at the back of her head as he fastened his mouth to hers. It was a punishing kiss. Toni's attempt to resist was futile, like pushing against a solid brick wall until finally he pulled back slightly. He didn't release her, but gave her all the room she needed to pull out of his arms, to escape the assault of his kiss. But she didn't.

Judd lifted his head just enough to look at her. She watched the anger in his eyes change to a ragged empathy, to pain, to desire, before he kissed her again taking her breath away. Swept with dizziness, she swayed into him, not realizing he had swept her up in his arms until he lifted his lips from hers to lay her gently on the office couch and came down hungrily on top of her, smothering her face with more kisses.

She was beyond any consequential thought, only a need to fulfill the inexperienced tormenting desire flooding her body. But somewhere inside of her, a *stop* rose up. A very clear *stop*. She knew that Guidance and she fought with herself to heed it.

"No, Judd. Let me go," she moaned softly.

He raised up to glare incredulously at his little willing captive. "There's nothing to stop us but a slight legal technicality and we can deal with that anytime," his tone was sensuously low.

No, something about this wasn't right. Despite the urging of her body to give it all to this cowboy, there was something good, something precious missing, a sweetness of real love that she believed would be tainted, never recaptured if she gave in now.

Toni cried out and pushed against his rock hard chest. "I can't do this."

The suddenness of his release surprised her, but the way he now stood looking down at her, his breath coming in hard uneven gasps, cold blue eyes sweeping her, fists clenching and unclenching at his sides, she was sure she would not leave this room in one whole piece, and yet she was not afraid of him. His nostrils flared with rage but he made no move to touch her again. "Get out of here before you get hurt."

Sickened at the disgusted way he had looked at her, it took some effort to steady herself when she got up. Her usual reserve was in shambles, but for some reason she couldn't leave yet. She needed something from him, but what? To hear him say, 'I'm sorry'? That the hate she'd seen in his eyes wasn't true?

She strained to collect her stability before speaking. Judd's back was to her and she hoped his relaxed stance meant he had cooled down. His long jeans-clad legs were heavily muscled matching the thick visible strength of his broad shoulders. His shirttail was only half tucked into the slim waist of his jeans. The man, she thought, was just that, all man. And she found herself trembling under her scrutiny of a man who had just given her every reason to despise him. Why didn't she? It would be so much easier to cope.

She was still staring at him when he suddenly turned around and ran a strange enigmatic expression over her flushed face, then spoke slowly, exaggerating every word.

"Well, now, what's this? Change your mind?"

She took a breath trying to sort out exactly what she did want. "Judd...I..."

"Skip it." He cut her off sharply. "It makes no difference now and after tomorrow it'll matter even less."

"Tomorrow?"

She watched him walk around behind his desk and retrieve a key from somewhere underneath the top drawer, open another drawer and quickly produce a wad of paper money. Counting out a small stack, he replaced part of it, then the key and came to her forcing the money into her hand.

"Two thousand dollars, Toni. It'll get you a start. I'll see you get to the airport tomorrow. Go pack your things."

Her head came up in shock. "I can't take this."

"Why not? You were willing to take it two days ago."

"And you made no bones about your thoughts on the subject."

"My thoughts haven't changed. Women are always eager to take from a man before kicking his guts out, so take it. But you can throw your punches at some ignorant fool down the road."

The fury trembling in the man before her was like none she'd seen yet and she took an involuntary step backward. If she wasn't sure a moment ago, she was now that she would never take one unearned dime from Judd Luke.

She could see him battling for control. Why if he felt such disgust for women, had he attempted to make love to her and more than that, dare to mention marriage for such a shallow reason. Surely what a few rangy cowboys thought wouldn't

SURRENDERED

matter *that* much. She made her position clear about the money, then walked past him and laid it on his desk.

"Toni, you hear me good. You're making a bed you may find difficult to lay in."

She flinched, but forced a careless twist on her mouth. "Thanks for the warning, Cowboy."

She walked out toward the kitchen and soon heard Judd close the front door softly behind himself. She drew herself a glass of water to drown the lump in her throat. Her heart beat furiously and she forced her chaotic thoughts to settle by dissolving herself in work and then fell physically and emotionally exhausted into bed as soon as darkness came.

But sleep was lost when her mind hassling over the situation returned. Regardless of how much pain he inflicted on her, an inner strength, stronger than she had been aware of before, held her emotionally in tack urging her to hold on, to wait, leaving a knowing deep inside that he somehow needed her.

In a strange way, history seemed to be repeating itself. A personal history that had ended years ago, leaving her very young heart in misunderstood pain. A pain that had soon disappeared. She had fancied herself in love with him then without any persuasion on his part. And the childish wanting of something she never knew had soon eased away.

She rolled onto her stomach in an effort to squash the jerking movements inside her, balling her pillow under her head with her arms. But, now she knew. She had experienced his touch, his gentleness, his brutality, the caresses of his flesh against hers. And she wanted more. She wanted him. The agony had all returned, but more severe now than the day it had brought a storm of weeping in Uncle John's hayloft.

Could she actually change so drastically within the space of a couple of days? And not even that. Something switched gears inside of her in a moment. That moment she had felt the strength of Cowboy's arms around her, his lips touching hers.

She felt her arm muscles throbbing under her pillow and realized her fists were clenched. Moaning softly, she sought distraction, got up and switched on the night light beside her bed, then walked to the dresser and picked up her hair brush. Feathering the soft brown locks away from her face, she studied her reflection in the mirror thinking how young she looked in her skimpy pajamas; more like a slumber party teen than the woman she would have to be to conquer the heart of a man like Judd.

She wondered then what his reaction would be if she marched straight to him and accepted his marriage proposal in her pjs. She wanted to laugh at that but couldn't.

Her thoughts were interrupted by a heavy thudding of footsteps outside her closed door. Her breathing all but stopped when the knob turned and the door opened to a crack.

"Toni?"

Her heart jerked. "Just a minute." She moved quickly toward the covers of her bed but not fast enough as the man's figure emerged into the faint light of the room.

She whipped around wide-eyed, unaware of the frightened little girl appearance she was displaying as color rushed to her cheeks. She stood hesitant to finish her journey only a couple feet away as Judd's eyes boldly moved the length of her. Her eye caught sight of an oblong box in his hand and she relaxed when he held it toward her, taking his gaze from her juvenile nighty.

"A gift." He looked tense and strained.

"Gift?" She looked at him in unbalanced disbelief.

"One dozen red roses. Read the card."

She took the open envelope and felt her mouth drop open as she read '*Congratulations Mr. And Mrs. Judd V. Luke*'. It was signed simply, 'The Double OO Boys.' She shook her head in disbelief, but her heart was thumping double time. "Good heavens. What have we done?"

"Where did you come up with the *we*?" he snapped.

She looked up into his face and shock jolted her when her eyes met his. They held none of the mockery his tone implied, but a strange detached amusement that discomposed her because it urged her to throw her arms around her Cowboy and tell him how she really felt. She glanced away instead but Judd reached and pinched the material of her pj top pulling gently until she stepped closer.

"Have you ever slept with a man, Toni?" he asked flatly, even though he knew the answer to that without asking.

The question stunned her but she managed to look squarely at him. "I thought you had that all figured out. Besides, you wanted to marry me to save face," she reminded him saucily. "I fail to see what my state of virginity has to do with that."

"Now there's a direct evasion if I've ever heard one."

"That wasn't an evasion. Just a simple none of your business," she challenged.

His eyes narrowed. "Which doesn't leave the conclusion to one's imagination, does it?"

She felt the rein on her anger snap. "Then I can hardly understand your wanting to marry me," she spat and slapped his hand away from her. She knew from the lines creasing his face that she was pushing the wrong buttons, but her anger overpowered and she pushed some more. "A man with such high and mighty morals!"

"Close your mouth, right now!" Judd's voice was deliberately low and too controlled.

"No, I won't!" She barreled ahead, too angry to heed the dark features of the man reaching for her, and barely controlling the urge to shake her. "Why, you're just liable to come home any time after a long hard day in the saddle and find the little wife rolling in the hay with a new man. Not that you'd care, of course, but what would the Double OO boys think?"

She hit her mark, regretting it immediately when his grip tightened.

He pushed her backward until the backs of her legs bumped something solid. Tears spilled on her cheeks and she cried out softly as she was tossed into a heap on her bed. "Oh dear Jesus," was all she heard before the door slammed hard and she released a storm of muffled sobs into her pillow. *Lord, where are you? You promised you would never leave me.*

The next moment, she opened her eyes to late morning. The night seemed to have passed in seconds. A strong scent of roses flooded her nostrils bringing back the sting of the past evening. She moaned and climbed out of bed wondering fleetingly how she'd managed to tuck the covers so neatly around her in her sleep and stared a little dumbfounded at the red roses arranged in a gallon size pickle jar against the foot of the bed.

She dressed hurriedly in jeans and a white V-neck T-shirt and almost groaned out loud when she stood in front of the mirror. There wasn't enough make-up in the world to fix that. She brushed her hair and padded barefoot down the hall to the bathroom. The cold water on her face helped, but the discovery that she was alone in the house helped more.

With a steaming cup of coffee in hand, she retreated to a propped pillow on her bed to try to produce some positive thoughts. She had acted on just one foolish whim, applying for her dream job, and bingo, disaster. But the misfortune was not because she was, by her own sense of independence, trapped and doomed to weeks of domestic drudgery, but because she knew, despite all, it would take something unthinkably cruel to erase the mark of Cowboy Luke from her heart. They were destiny's marks impressed upon her years before, returning now to complete the cycle. Maybe she was being over-dramatic, but somewhere there was a sweet, loving Cowboy hidden beneath a covering of a dreadful experience. And she knew she had some divine part to play in his rescue. God help her, even if it meant marrying him for reputation's sake to fulfill it.

She swallowed a mouthful of hot coffee and closed her eyes against the tender throb in her arms. It wasn't Cowboy who had inflicted that pain, but this strange bruised part of him reacting to a harsh secret memory, one that her uncontrolled temper had obviously opened. A lump swelled her throat as she wondered almost fearfully who the woman was.

"Well," she sighed to the light of a half gone day. "This is not getting any work done."

She began work in her own room, vowing to start fresh. A spirited determination was a woman's best ally and all she needed was a good yank on her boot straps and a little good humor. Ok. Maybe a truck load of good humor.

She moved the *redneck* arrangement of roses to the bedside table for a finishing touch, then noticed the ashtray on the floor on the far side of the table. She distinctly remembered washing it yesterday, yet it contained one cigarette that looked like it had been lit, then immediately snuffed out. She felt her stomach quiver knowing he had tucked her under the blankets while she slept. She smiled.

***

CHAPTER FOUR

Toni's thoughts were on Cowboy, even though she tried to concentrate on cleaning. After a few days, the entire ranch house took on new life, even a pleasant, clean smell. Toni was a little surprised when she bothered to walk through and look at the results of her labor.

She hadn't seen Cowboy since the night he pickle-jarred the roses. The only inkling that he had come home at all was finding his bed covers rumpled in the mornings and dirty clothes piled on the laundry room floor. She decided that he must have come to his senses and pulled back his marriage demands. Just how he intended to fix that information with his ranch hands was anybody's guess, but she was sure he could come up with something survivable for himself. She had enough on her mind at present just trying to stay busy enough and tired enough to ease her longing for the ranch boss's presence. But that longing was soon turning into a feeling of rejection. Then anger at herself for letting a virtual stranger have an inroad into her emotions this way. After nearly a week, the deep cleaning was caught up and the lonely isolation was barely tolerable.

Out of desperation one afternoon, she showered and slipped on some cowboy duds. She clamped her hair up on either side with a pair of silver twisted-wire berets, a special gift from Uncle John on her graduation night.

Her eyes misted remembering the emotion that had shook Uncle John's big cracked and calloused hands when he had handed her the tiny unwrapped box. 'For my little cowgirl,' he'd choked out. She smiled at her visual memory of him, then bounded out the back door as if the house was burning behind her.

The sun was bright with only a casual breeze to cool it down. A little bird was somewhere in the huge tree overhead loudly declaring her presence. Probably one of Judd's spies, she mused. The thought caused her to glance around guiltily. This was still work hours but she'd be sure to make it up somewhere. It appeared she was alone, so she relaxed and walked to the empty arena feeling a hungry stirring for the life she sorely missed. She climbed the rails and easily let herself down into the deep sand.

A familiar faced man stepped into view from inside the barn opening at the far end of the arena. From a distance he looked so much like her uncle, she sucked a quick breath.

"Afternoon, Mrs. Luke." He waved a greeting.

Mrs. Luke? "Oh, hello." Her heart twisted.

"Nice to see you out and around. Judd said you was a little under the weather."

Well, he was explaining things away nicely so far, she thought, walking towards the man. "Thank you. It's such a gorgeous day."

"Sure is that all right. Name's Sky Cooper."

Toni shook his hand, finally recognizing him as the man who had opened the front door the day she arrived at the ranch.

"Just Toni."

He nodded, flicking an approving smile at her. "Well, Judd's got himself a mighty pretty little wife. It ain't no wonder he posted a couple extra hands close in to watch the comings and goings of the house. Can't tell who might straggle up. Some cagey characters roamin' around these days."

Her lids flew up but the older man excused himself back to work before she could find her tongue. Was Judd really concerned for her safety? Or was he afraid she'd hang a red light on the front door.

She climbed up and perched on the top rail of the arena at Sky's suggestion when he emerged from the barn riding a high headed little filly. Only green-broke, she pranced one way, then another, tossing a buck now and then.

Toni forgot Judd and his spies and concentrated on how she could persuade Sky to let her ride. Then she remembered. He could hardly refuse Mrs. Judd V. Luke. She jumped into the soft sand wondering what the V. stood for and motioned Sky to dismount. He did so quickly, frowning as he held the fidgety animal at arm's length.

"I'd like to ride her, if you don't mind."

The man's eyes popped in disbelief. "No mam. Not this one. She's barely broke."

"I can handle her. Besides, being married to the boss sort of entitles me, wouldn't you say." Toni reached around for the reins, but he stepped in front of her, agitation on his face.

"Maybe you'd better wait for Judd."

"He knows I can ride. I'm sure he won't think a thing of it."

Reluctantly, Sky did as she asked and Toni felt sorry for what she could see she was putting him through. But it was now or never. Judd would never consent to this. He wouldn't give her the time of day.

The filly's ears worked constantly, her eyes showing their whites at Toni's approach. The colt quivered and stiffened slightly, but allowed the stranger's touch. She let Toni rub her hand along her neck and down her shoulder without trying to step away. As Toni murmured softly to her, the little sorrel's eyes softened, her body language signaling that Toni was welcome.

"Hey, pretty girl," she said as she touched the soft velvet muzzle voluntarily offered to her. The filly remained watchful, but relaxed, seeming to feel an immediate rapport with her new handler. Toni sensed immediately that this baby had been handled correctly from the start, trusting new people easily. The young horse hooked up with her soft voice quickly enough, but Toni knew it was mostly in the eyes. It sees a soft eye or hard eye and goes on alert when a less than peaceful spirit approaches.

The first hint of flight eased away as Toni spoke to her by voice and eye contact simultaneously. She continued to rub the neck and face, sliding her open hand softly across the filly's eye, first one and then the other. Horses received that hand to eye glide as a kiss. Her eyelid closed for the contact as she dipped her head slightly in relaxed contentment, the kiss returned. Toni dropped her hands and the reins and backed up several steps. The pony followed her, nudging her midsection with its nose, asking for more.

Finally after a measure of trust was established between the pair, Toni took up the reins again and eased herself up in one stirrup, letting the filly feel her weight. Then in one fluid move, she was in the saddle. The filly turned her head around as far as her neck would stretch and made a soft murmuring noise that a colt would make to its mother. Toni's lips moved, but only the filly could hear her reply.

Sky watched with awe and an immediate respect for this young woman who obviously knew her way around a green broke colt. He wasn't surprised now to watch her body move with the rhythm of the horse, riding in relaxed, perfect form.

The aging wrangler backed up against the rails of the pen shaking his head, barely believing what he was seeing. He'd watched it happen in lesser degree many times between cowboys and their horses. Across Montana, Wyoming,

Colorado and Texas, in the mountains, desert, foothills and rivers, but never witnessed the romantic drama he was watching now between cowgirl and horse.

He could see she was experienced enough and thought nothing of it when she caught his eye as she trotted around in front of him and nodded toward the gate, indicating she wanted to ride outside. He quickly complied taking only a few seconds to get his stiff joints moving across the pen and swung open the gate.

Toni had almost forgotten how free she felt astride a horse. Any horse. Like being let out of a cage. She held the reins low and against the colt's neck, careful to keep her legs out of its touchy sides.

It dawned on Toni that this was the first time since the day Uncle John died that she had felt a breeze blow her hair from the back of a horse. Tears filled her eyes as a flare of joy imploded within her. She suddenly felt fourteen and indestructible. The little filly kicked her back legs out in reply to her rider's hi-yi vibes, bringing a burst of laughter from Toni.

The vastness of space and majestic mountains and blue sage valleys cedars and Aspens spread in every direction. Could the Creator of this earthly Heaven have felt the same burst of *wow* as when He said *"let there be?"* No doubt.

Toni rode in silent awe for, she guessed, a couple of miles. She had deliberately set out on a more westerly trek and relished the subtle change of scenery. The pastureland began to gently roll with thick dark green grasses and clusters of pines dotting the hillsides. She realized she was inside of the foothills of the Wind River mountain range, part of Wyoming's claim to the Great Rockies. She had read about this beautiful country a few weeks ago. Now, here she sat, horseback, and surrounded by more breathtaking beauty than her imagination had ever shown her.

The pair meandered through gentle valleys and canyons before intercepting a cattle trail that headed toward the thickness of tall pines. She rode into the trees listening to a bird whistle mingled with a rustle of wind in the branches. Soon she exited the trees into a clearing that was obviously man-made. She turned her head and stared for a full silent minute at a gate entrance about fifty yards ahead of her. The lavishness of it would seem out of place except the tasteful décor fit right in with the wilderness landscape.

Two large wagon wheels were inset into the middle of roughhewn rock walls and adorned with heavily polished pine log railing above each wall. The rustic gates were made from the same polished railing and stood wide open. *Wow*, was all she could think.

She moved her pony forward to get a better view of the ritzy entrance. Head tilted back, she squinted at the massive gleaming log crossbar that towered high above the full length of the gates. Suddenly she couldn't move or breathe or stop staring. Burned into the monster log in beautiful script was LUKE. The beauty of this majestic piece of art made the discovery a pleasant surprise, but a strange one, considering the untamed country she had just ridden through. One minute she was moving through uninhabited canyons, believing she had left civilization behind; the next she was sitting at an entrance to...? That was a good question. To where?

Cowboy obviously had family she didn't know about. In truth, she knew nothing about him, except that she loved him.

Curiosity moved her through the inviting gates and for the first time she noticed the rough cut road that lead way from the gate and through another thickness of trees. There must be a main road close by, she surmised as she tapped the filly with the heel of her boot and trotted up the path. Uphill went for at least a quarter of a mile. As she topped the peak, a deep breath sucked almost unconsciously into her lungs.

Toni stared in fascination and surprise at the log and stone mountain style villa. It seemed to have appeared out of nowhere, sitting like an artist's masterpiece a couple hundred yards in front of her, yet blending as though it was birthed by the natural soft hues of the very land it set on. She could tell it hadn't been there long. But what *Luke* did it belong to?

She wanted to ride up for a better look, but her attention was arrested by the low westerly shadows playing across the narrow road in front of her.

"Oh good heavens," she mumbled after glancing at her Timex. She had been out of sight of the ranch for hours.

The filly perked her ears, then turned one backward, respectfully listening in on her rider's comment.

"Sky's going to call out a posse if we don't get home." Reluctantly, she decided this adventure would have to wait for another day. She turned and backtracked through the trees like she had come and picked up the pace.

0   After a half hour or so, Toni realized the scenery had changed. Or maybe it just looked different going in the opposite direction. Had she rode through that narrow pass between the canyon walls? She didn't remember. The choice to go right or left was a coin toss. The horizon was the same on all sides. For all the exhilaration that she had felt on the ride out here, a despairing apprehension was leading her back. Toni had no idea whether she was going in the right direction or not. She didn't know if she was aimed for the ranch or a night alone with the prairie dogs.

0   The land rolled until she couldn't glimpse sight of the mountains on any horizon. She was convinced now that she'd made the wrong choice as she trotted across an unfamiliar canyon floor and up into a cradle of rocks and thorny brush, then stopped. Surprised at the sight of glistening aspens just in front of her, Toni turned in her saddle to glance behind and as she did, a shadow darkened the space overhead. A huge grayish bird suddenly dropped from the top of the trees into the brush beside them, then flapped heavily to retreat. Horse and rider instinctively stiffened from the unexpected visitor.

Everything happened so fast that Toni wasn't fully sure exactly what *did* happen. Her breath left her lungs for a few seconds as she struggled to move. Something was jabbing into her shoulder. She was sprawled like a pretzel in a clump of trees and realized that her mount had bolted and turned out from under her.

She lay there thinking she should get up, but she couldn't seem to get started. She looked around. The filly was long gone.

Then it began. A gut tightening pain ripped through her upper back and left arm.

Oh great! Well this is a fine how-do-you-do. She moaned and willed herself to not cry. The pain was becoming unbearable, pulling low moaning growls out of her throat. She tried to think about what she should do, but had trouble hearing her own thoughts. Was she passing out?   No. She felt too much pain for that luxury.

Fear suddenly rushed up on her like a cold wind. She had ridden several miles straight out into only God knew where. And here she lay, hidden in a tree line, can't move and nobody had a clue.

Guilt mushroomed in her thoughts until she felt it tighten her chest. Judd would soon be searching for her, probably along with Sky and maybe others. They would lose hours of work because of her.

She focused her eyes straight up into the late evening sky. *Jesus, couldn't you just zap me back together right fast before Judd finds me? I'm pretty sure grave yard dead will be putting it mildly if he gets here first.*

"Oooh," she whimpered against the back, shoulder and arm pain. Her left arm was obviously broken and she wasn't sure what else.

Thank You. Yes, thank You. The pain seemed to be draining away. She closed her eyes and enjoyed the relief. When she opened them again it was dark and cold and the pain was worse.

Something small rustled in the undergrowth close by. As long as it didn't sound any bigger than that, she'd let it stay.

"Oh Judd. Where are you? Please find me." She could barely hear herself whisper. She felt only a breath away from panicking suddenly. *Don't you dare lose it now, Toni Barton,* she threatened herself. *God sent you to this ranch. He won't leave you for bear bait. Bear bait?* "You won't, will You?" She voiced into the darkness in a loud whisper. *I hope the snakes have gone to bed. No. Don't think, don't think.*

It was worse than eerie, waiting, unable to move. She wondered how long she'd been passed out. She wondered what Cowboy was thinking right now. *Better not to know that! What I'd give for a drink of water.* Tears burned her eyes, then tickled her cheeks as they spilled over.

The sun was hanging very westerly when Sky led a big roan gelding out of the barn and started tracking out of the ranch yard. His heart jumped into his throat, finishing off the apprehension he'd felt the past hour when he spotted Judd trotting across the meadow on his bay cutter with the little sorrel filly ponied behind him.

It was obvious by Judd's halfcocked grin that he thought the filly got loose from him in the arena.

"Hey, old man," Judd teased him, even while his eyes traveled over him searching for a sign of injury. "Lose something. Or did something lose you?"

When the gap closed between the horses, Judd's bantering turned at the sight of Sky's worried expression. "Sky, you hurt, buddy?"

"No. Where'd you pick her up at?" He nodded toward the filly.

"Grazing in the valley below my tent."

"Toni was riding her, Judd. She's been gone going on four hours. I got busy and time got away from me before I realized she'd been gone too long."

Judd's face paled, questions popping one after the other in his head, but he shoved them to the back burner for the time being.

"Which way did she head out?" His easy tone defied the fear pounding in his chest.

"Last I saw, she disappeared over that far bluff." Sky pointed toward the mountains.

Judd handed the filly's reins to Sky. "Put her up, then ride to the holding pens on the back ninety and get the boys. All of 'em. Head them in her direction." He wheeled the bay around and sunk his spurs. Somebody would answer for this stunt. And he figured he knew right where to start asking questions...as soon as he caught up with her.

He rode through one sage brush canyon, then another, calling her name and scouting for tracks, guessing which way was the right one. After nearly an hour of nothing, he felt fear like he hadn't felt before. *Why would she ride this far? Didn't she know the dangers...the bears, mountain lions...?* He shut off his thoughts before he got sick.

A plume of dust rose up from the east trailing Sky and the other cowboys as they raced to catch up with him. Judd took Sky and backtracked, yelling Toni's name around every rock and bend in the canyon. *She wouldn't have gone farther than this!*

The other eight spread out two by two. Judd and Doyle Williamson both carried shotguns in a scabbard on their saddles. One shot would signal that she'd been found.

Worry and anger twisted together in Judd's gut. He wanted to ask Sky how Toni had managed to be on that filly. He wanted to ask *her* why she was foolish enough to go so far into wild country like this. He didn't know the why about this mess, but he *did* know the answer to another dilemma. And as soon as he got her safely back to the ranch, he would see that he corrected the situation immediately.

He took a deep breath fighting off panic now. Darkness had fallen. *Sweet Jesus, help me. He couldn't remember ever seriously calling on Jesus before now. Toni. Where are you?* Judd had successfully erected a sturdy fort around his heart, at least since he'd been old enough to recognize that the greatest anguish in his life had been inflicted by women. The walls could not be breached, but somehow he'd stupidly managed to leave the gates unbolted. And somehow, this little spitfire of a cowgirl had taken hold of the most private and protected area in the fort. His heartstrings.

Judd felt his stomach knot up tighter. He knew all too well the dangers that lurked out here and the thought of Toni being hurt or...worse made him almost feel faint. He swallowed at the growing lump in his throat. He was in love with her. Maybe he always had been. He thought of his dad. Felt confused. Nothing in his well-ordered life made a dime's worth of sense anymore.

He cursed himself with every step his horse took. He should never have left her alone these past days. He knew for a fact she was a naïve young woman in the ways of loving a man. Or being loved by one. He knew he had scared her. Damn his hot tempered hide. He had forced her to stay at the ranch. Not to be mean to her. But because his heart had done a teenaged style flip flop the moment he had laid eyes on her that morning standing in his den. He just didn't know what to do with it at the time.

Regardless of what had happened here today, he felt fully responsible. More than that. He felt cut to the quick in his gut at the thought that he might not have the chance to show her the real Judd Luke. For some reason, what he felt inside himself never seemed to make it to the outside where it could be seen. He dragged a gloved hand down his face attempting to release taut nerves. *Don't give up on me yet,* he prayed silently, not sure if he was directing that to God or Toni.

A shotgun blast suddenly filled the moonlit earth.

Judd shouted at Sky who rode a few yards from him. "That came from the timber line."

The entire search party headed toward the mountains, all with their hearts in their throats.

In minutes, Judd had swung down from his saddle and was leaning over Toni where she was sprawled in the clump of brush and saplings and rocks.

"She's alive, Judd, but don't move her." It was Doyle who had taken off his grimy blue plaid shirt and gently laid it over her cold body.

"Toni, baby. Can you hear me?" He ripped the buttons from his denim shirt getting it off and added it to Doyle's, gently tucking it around her. Five more stinky work shirts were ripped off, each cowboy handing his in turn to Judd. He lowered his head and swallowed hard.

A soft whimper sounded in Toni's throat, but she didn't open her eyes.

Judd's insides turned painfully at the sight of her small, fragile body curled up in a mess of blood and sticks and dirt and smelly shirts and not be able to pick her up in his arms and make her know she was safe.

Doyle kept a hand on Judd's shoulder in a gesture of comfort. "Help's on the way, Judd. Les and A.J. radioed for Medi-Vac to come fly her out of here."

Judd felt of her head, his throat going dry when he felt a large goose egg in the back. "She hit her head. Her arm's broken." He seemed to be talking more to himself than the others.

Toni heard voices way off in the distance. Find...me. Cowboy?"

Thank God. "I'm here, Toni. Don't try to move. We'll have you out of here in a few minutes." He rubbed the back of his hand up and down on her cheek, and swallowed a fresh swell in his throat.

0   Somebody handed him a bedroll from behind the cantle of their saddle. "Thanks," he said without looking up, and draped it on top of the shirts.

"Thirsty…water." Toni's voice was thick and dry.

"Got some coming," he lied, knowing full well he couldn't give her any. "Where's that blasted helicopter?

It seemed like eternity had come and gone before the helicopter was finally on its way to Jackson with Toni strapped solidly to a back board.

The ranch was dark and silent when Judd and Sky arrived, much the same as the ride back had been. Neither man chose to intrude on the other's weary frustrations with questions or explanations. Time and place for everything.

After bedding down the horses, Sky headed for the bunkhouse after Judd assured the older cowboy that he in no way held him responsible for Toni's lack of good judgment. Sky Cooper was a kind, gentle soul. Judd thought many times it would be a good thing to strive to be more like him. Hurting that old gent would be akin to slicing his own heart out. It wasn't going to happen.

Toni had been x-rayed and prepared for setting her broken arm when Judd arrived at the hospital. He signed the paperwork waiting for him and let out a long, easy breath when the doctor told him her worst injury was the arm. She'd taken a good bang on the back of her head with a stout tree limb, but they'd keep a close eye on her at the hospital for a few days. Other than a few scratches, jabs and bruises, she'd just be sore for a while.

"Mr. Luke, would you like to see your wife before we take her to surgery? She's been asking for you." A nurse in surgical scrubs held open one side of a set of double doors.

My wife. He nodded and stepped past her, hat in hand and waited for her to lead the way.

Judd stood in the door of the E.R. and watched for Toni's eyes to spot him. *God help me. She's beautiful.* His wife, who was *not* his wife, was wrapped like a package of meat in white gauze bandages, blood still smeared in places and matted in her hair. An I.V. was inserted in a vein in the back of her hand. *If I'd lost you, lady, it would have killed me.*

She looked at him.

"So, which was it?" he asked her, flat toned.

She looked confused. "Was...what?"

"I can see you've been on the bottom half of a stampede. Just wondered if it was cattle or buffalo?"

She attempted a smile. "Don't make...me laugh. It would kill me...all over."

Yeah. Been there. Judd walked to her bedside and bent down to lay a gentle peck on her lips. His arms were throbbing with a desire to grab her up and hold her tight against him. With his lips close to her ear, he whispered, "You ever scare me like that again, your butt's mine!"

He stood back up and she saw blue eyes that held no derision, but a compassionate fear and gentleness. Her eyes swam, but the pain shooting through her body was only a secondary reason.

The first thing she recalled after waking from surgery was Cowboy's farewell quip as he had bent down and kissed her quickly on the cheek just before she was wheeled behind the surgery doors, "Some women will do anything to get out of washing windows." She smiled at the remembrance and fell asleep.

Two days later, Toni was ready to leave the hospital. She woke that morning to find Cowboy occupying a straight backed chair across the room. He wore new jeans and a crisp white long sleeved western shirt that looked new as well. His black hair was clean and silky beneath a silver belly Stetson she hadn't seen before.

"Morning, sleeping beauty."

"Hi." His Sunday best appearance seemed to magnify her need to clean up. "I can take a hint," she groaned for emphasis. "I'll see if I can manage a quick shower before we go."

"No need for that. I've already bailed you out of here."

Toni winced at his intolerant tone.

It then dawned on her that she couldn't work and there was not one reason she could invent to keep her on at the Double OO. So much for the warm hand of destiny, she thought, then closed her eyes against the stinging swell of salt water.

She opened her eyes again to find him standing beside the bed.

"Is the pain bad?" He studied her expression, concern clouding his face.

"Never felt better in my life. Like you said, there's more than one way to get out of a nasty job," she popped back. In truth, her heart was aching almost beyond endurance.

The door opened then as a nurse came through handing Judd another form to sign. She smiled sweetly at Toni. "From what I've heard, Mrs. Luke, luck was in your back pocket a few days ago. As soon as your husband signs that, you're free to go. I'll help you get dressed."

Toni stared blankly a moment, stunned. Who had said Judd was her husband? "I...I...," she couldn't think.

"Thank you," Judd nodded, handing back the signed paper. "I can manage to get her ready."

"Alright, but you take it easy for a few days, honey." She patted the bed smiling. "Here's a prescription for pain meds. She'll need them for a few more days." She handed the slip of paper to Judd. "Take care now," she said to the door on her way out.

Toni turned disbelieving eyes on Judd's masterful smirk.. "Would you mind telling me what's going on?"

"Did you bang your head in the fall or don't you remember? You're my wife."

"But, I'm *not* your wife!"

"Oh?" His eyebrows rose tauntingly. "Well, maybe Sky Cooper misunderstood you."

"Sky Cooper! You're the one who made the big announcement to your ranch hands."

"And you had no qualms about informing him of what being married to the ranch boss entitled you to." His features sharpened teasingly.

She caught her breath. "Oh, that," was all she could manage.

She watched him retrieve a plastic bag from the floor and pull out a long white silk gown and matching robe. It was the richest gown she'd even been given. The tags were still hanging from the sleeve. Toni was genuinely touched at his thoughtfulness.

He draped it across the foot of the bed, then proceeded to help her to a sitting position. A cool draft touched her back and she froze, realizing she only wore an open-backed hospital wrap. With her good arm, she reached around to close the gap, but Judd was already pulling on the tie at the back to release it.

Color scorched her face. "I can manage it myself." She made an involuntary move to stop him and moved her plastered arm. The maddening pain shot a gasp and a moan from her throat.

"Good God, woman, sit still before you break the thing over again."

Her heart hammered ferociously and she just managed to slap her hand to her chest catching the wrap before it fell. She couldn't look at Judd, but knew instinctively that he was smiling above her head.

Slowly she relaxed as he gently stretched the new gown over her cast, then slipped it over her head. His fingers brushed the skin of her neck in the process and she trembled, the commanding maleness of him so powerful her nerves tumbled in spasms. She was surprised when she stepped to the floor that her knees would hold her. She slipped her arm in a robe sleeve and Judd draped the other side over her shoulder.

Only then did she notice the matching white silk slippers beside her feet. She scooted into them as Judd effortlessly snapped the tag from the gown.

"All set?" he asked, holding her upper arm as if he thought she might fall on her face.

She glanced around the room. "I did have clothes on when I came here."

"I took them home. But I'm afraid the blouse didn't survive. They had to cut it off of you."

Home. She wanted to throw herself down somewhere and cry.

Once in the truck, Toni took a fresh hold of her herself. Her conscience smarted with the burden she had laid on Judd and even though she could hardly bear the thought of leaving, she knew the sooner she did, the sooner she could begin piecing herself back together. She cleared her throat, praying that her tears would hold up until after the final goodbye because in all likelihood, it would be a downpour.

Judd?" she said huskily.

He looked at her and she felt herself swim with the agony of wanting him.

"We have to talk...about this."

"I'm listening."

God, did he have to sound so gentle. "A...about the money you offered me...before. Am I still good for a loan? It'll be awhile, but I can eventually pay it back."

"A loan? What for?" His expression was paltry.

"What for? Well, obviously I can't work for a few weeks and I can't expect you to turn the ranch into a nursing home for crippled hitchhikers."

He laughed. "You're absolutely right. I just happen to have a one way ticket to Timbuktu in my hip pocket. For all you've got going for you in Dallas, you may as well use it. Shall I drop you at the bus depot?"

"Very funny. You can at least give me time to dress and get my stuff."

"I could, but I'm pressed for time right now. There is one alternative, however."

It dawned on her then that Judd had pulled the truck to a stop along a residential street. He switched off the motor and turned toward her, draping his arm along the back of the seat.

"Why did you stop here?" She was distrustfully puzzled.

"This is your alternative."

Toni almost laughed then despite herself. "It's babies they leave on doorsteps, Cowboy." She did laugh then as her mind formed an image of a woman in a white nightie standing at someone's door with a hardship note taped to her broken arm.

When she regained her composure, she saw Judd looking at her and smiling almost fondly and she strained to keep from throwing her good arm around him.

"You look just like John when you laugh like that," he grinned broadly, straight, white pearls caressing his outrageous good looks.

"Well, maybe you'd better explain this new plan to me."

"Same old plan I had before. Marry me."

Had he reached out and slapped her she couldn't have been more astounded. "Marry you! Here? Now? Like this?" She felt like she was in the front car of a run-away roller coaster.

"Yes, mam. Here and now and just as you are. A retired justice of the peace lives here and we have an appointment of which we're five minutes late already."

"You can't be serious." Her eyes were opened so wide they hurt. "Anyway, it takes license and things."

"Ah, I nearly forgot. Here in my other hip pocket I just happen to have one that's been collecting dust for a couple days."

"But...how did you...?"

"Closed-mouth friends in high places. It's legal."

"But, Judd, I...we...." It's what she wanted all along, to conquer the one love of her life, to have him to love forever. But her mind was a wild confusion of hope and fear knowing she hadn't really conquered anything. He had never professed to care a wit for her, only his saintly image. Could she dare to hope he would ever really love her? She remembered her vow to make him love her in time, a prayer she might have mumbled in a fit of passion, and here it was... a lifetime laid out before her. She was petrified.

"It's I Do or Timbuktu. The choice is yours."

Her face lifted to his bluntness and in the steady fusion of her eyes with his, she saw a hint of need, of a yearning deep beneath the blue polished surface. She glimpsed the Cowboy she loved so hopelessly. And at that moment she decided she was crazy beyond all help.

"How many brides would you say have been to the alter in their nighties before now?" Her smile teased him and she was pleased at the sparkle that popped in Judd's eyes.

"Or without their underwear?" he laughed aloud. "Who can tell, you may be the founder of a whole new line in bridal attire."

The couple entered the dimly lighted entrance hall when the heavy wooden door was opened by a little gray haired woman who didn't look a day over eighty. Toni could tell they were expected but the quick intake of breath and disgusted once-over greeted her by the slightly hunched-backed lady momentarily screwed up her courage. But when she felt Judd's arm slip around her waist and her glance caught him looking down at her with an affectionate twinkle, she lifted her chin and smiled.

Follow me, please," the woman squeaked, shuffling ahead of them through a large living room that resembled a trinket shop and into a small study.

The aged gentleman who was about to pronounce a benediction that would change her life forever stood up from a tiny desk in the corner and came forward for a quick introduction and to shake hands.

Toni saw the startled look that appeared for a moment in the wrinkled face when his glance dropped for a split second on her wedding gown, then proceeded with a twinkle in his eyes to get to the task at hand. He briefly studied the marriage license Judd handed him and they were both startled when the old peace justice jerked his head up and smiled broadly at them.

"Of course! Of course! I should have caught it before." He was looking at Judd. "You're J.V.'s boy. Why I've known Jackson Luke since he was a young man. Fact was, your mama and daddy stood in my chambers in the courthouse and I married them some thirty, forty years ago. Pretty little thing your mama was, too. Just like your young lady here." He winked at Toni.

Judd's mother? The remark made Toni realize just how little she knew about Judd Luke.

"Yes sir, been ten year since I last saw J.V." The old man continued. "Sure sorry to hear he passed."

"Thank you." Judd said too stiffly and Toni looked up at him remembering Judd's father hadn't been dead a month yet. Was that what he had been trying to deal with, the emotional stress of his father's death?

"Now, if you two young folks are ready, I'll get you married so you can get on your way."

Judd held her unbound right hand and she tried desperately to forgive him for his sudden cold austerity. And even though she was so fully and painfully aware of the circumstances surrounding this marriage, Toni wondered why the too quick kiss only a moment after becoming the man's lifetime partner was so cruelly devastating to her.

Nothing would ever be quite the same for her, Toni realized during the ride...home. The fifteen minute ceremony couldn't have been more impersonal, but the delicate little diamond band circling the ring finger of her left hand would remind her constantly that it had happened. She was, in truth, Mrs. Judd Vincent Luke and she hadn't even known her husband's full name until a few minutes ago. The thought that someday she might wish she'd never heard his name at all made her shrink further into herself than what Judd's abrupt cold acceptance of her hand in marriage had already done. She wondered again, could the mere mention of his father's death turn him so zombie-like?

She looked at the solid lean form sitting an arm's reach from her, concentrating too deliberately on the nearly deserted road a short distance from the ranch. The last word to pass his lips was "I will," and he'd said it to an old man holding a Bible in front of them. It was as if the morning just past, their light conversation and laughter had never happened.

Suddenly she yearned to see him smile again. Anything to give her some impression that he wasn't sorely regretting that he didn't leave her a way out of this farce of a union.

"So," she exclaimed loudly, as she spread her fingers wide apart to display her ring finger. His startled expression faced her. "Does this little jewel make me head window washer...or what?"

He didn't laugh, but pursed his lips in agitation. "You don't deserve an answer to that, but I'll give you one. That little jewel makes it right for you to remain living with me. You *will* remain until you recover, then you can pick up on your life where it should have been left in the first place. Answer your question?" Bitterness had consumed him.

She dropped her hand and sat staring at him numbly. All she could seem to think of was the difficulty she had in keeping her body from visibly shaking. She couldn't take her eyes from him. She could see no small sign of her gentle Cowboy, but a hard, ruthless sort of man...her husband that she knew nothing about.

Silently she threw a blameful dart at Uncle John for so successfully teaching her to stick her neck out for whatever she wanted. 'Grab hold of your dream and never let go', he'd said. But she quickly withdrew the blame and draped it bitterly around her own shoulders. Uncle John had taught her a good thing. She was the one who had made a mockery of it.

"I said, does that answer your question?" he repeated sharply.

"You bet", she smiled palely. "It's your party. You choose the games."

His eyes widened on her and the sudden wicked slant of his mouth shot a dizzying thought through her mind. She understood his expression and turned to lock a stare out of her side window. At this moment she didn't know how she felt about it. About their marriage bed. If Judd wanted to make love to her, he was within his legal rights now. But even though she'd married him, knowing he didn't love her, allowing him to take total possession of her body out of no more than animal lust was another thing. She couldn't imagine giving her body to any man except Cowboy, but the chemistry between them had to change.

Well, there was one persuasive point she could make to stop it and she silently praised God for her bruised and broken body.

***

CHAPTER FIVE

Weary and weak, Toni allowed herself to be steered from the flatbed truck into the guest bedroom. She stood watching as Judd jerked back the covers on the bed, a little surprised that her eyelids were so heavy. She didn't object when he reached to slip the robe from her shoulders, her cares lost suddenly in a dizzying swoon.

"Easy." He wrapped a steady arm around her and when the spinning room slowed to a stop, she felt his fingers pressed tightly against her breast. He mistook her sudden tremble as a sign that she wasn't back to herself yet and increased the pressure of his hold. The thin film of silk beneath his hands felt like it was on fire. Every nerve in his body popped as he stroked her tousled hair and ran his spread fingers down her back. It felt so good to touch her like this. He wanted to touch her, *his wife*, every part of her at once. His blood pounded like a war drum.

"Better now?" He asked after a minute, his tone as calm as he could make it.

She could only nod, embarrassed, and yet, craving more of the cause for the sudden swelled tightness beneath his hand. And she was worried about how she would allay *his* privileged passions!

"Let's get you into bed and a pill down you. It's total bed rest for you for a few days."

Toni wiggled between the cool sheets as his hand gently guarded her plastered arm. He jerked up the extra pillow across the bed and cushioned it gently under her cast. Without a word he walked out returning in only a moment with a glass of water. He slipped his hand behind her neck and tilted her up enough to take a sip and down a pain capsule that she had begun to need.

Closing her eyes against a stab of pain in her arm, she was surprised to find him gone when she opened them again.

She sighed heavily, glad to be alone because she had the wildest impulse to roll onto her face and cry like a baby. But she wouldn't. Never would she permit Judd Vincent Luke to see traces of tears on her face again, to know how terribly he could crush her spirit. And besides, she couldn't roll over.

As the pill did its work, drowsiness relaxed her muscles and she allowed it to take her into a soothing nothingness.

Toni's first reaction was to scoot backward when she awakened to a large hand pressing her cheek, but she wasn't allowed to move. Judd's hands held firmly to her shoulders. When her eyes focused clearly, she realized with a jolt of surprise that he was smiling.

"What...what do you want," she stammered, still groggy.

"Now just what do you think I want my stubborn little bride?"

Her stomach knotted partly because she felt like she'd been hit by a truck and more partly because she wanted him to slide under the covers with her.

"No, Judd. I mean...I mean..." she twisted and he took his hands from her and stood up. During the minute it took for his laughter to fade away, Toni saw in the dimness of the night light that he only wore tan pajama bottoms. His upper torso was bare, his broad chest matted with curls of black hair. She fought inwardly to stop her aroused quivers hoping he hadn't noticed.

"It's time for your pill. I just touched you to be sure you hadn't developed a fever."

Toni's cheeks flushed swiftly and she wiggled to a sitting position. "You could have turned on a better light and awakened me first."

"Yeah, I could have." He grinned almost wickedly.

He's enjoying all this, she thought angrily, but the blue eyes now half hidden by lowered lids gave his brawny face a self-indulgent look that said he was considering more poking a pill down her.

Then, Toni realized *she* was enjoying that consideration and looked away quickly.

"I think maybe it's time we get something straight, Mrs. Luke." The sharp tone brought her eyes back up to him. The smile was gone and he stood taller. "I have every right to do as I please, including toss you into my bed, or crawl into yours.

And if and when I feel a need for a woman, I'll let you know without leaving room for misunderstanding of intentions."

Her chest tightened until she thought she'd suffocate. "For God sake, why did you force this marriage? Why, when you hate me so much?" She felt her anger rising, not sure whether to aim it at him or herself. "Your precious reputation had nothing to do with it. Such a cold blooded man like you wouldn't care what anyone else thinks."

Suddenly, he stepped closer, reaching for the glass of water and a capsule. "Here, swallow this." Her *cold blooded man* had stung like a slap across his face, but he sucked it up and did what he had come to do.

She downed the pill.

"Are you hungry? You missed supper."

"No." She couldn't look up at him but relaxed at his calmer tone.

She heard him expel a long sigh just before turning off the lamp. A haze of moonlight filtered across the room and she watched his shadowy image move to the door before he stopped and propped one outstretched arm against the frame and stared back at her in the silence. Then he broke the stillness, speaking in a quiet tenderness that squeezed her heart.

"It wasn't force. There's any number of things you could have done to prevent the ceremony from taking place. But you didn't. And just for your records, I do not hate you."

She didn't see him leave. She couldn't see anything through the combination of darkness and blinding tears that ran in streams down her face. So much for her 'no more tears' resolution, she thought almost contentedly.

She awoke just before dawn and watched the morning break in soft shades of orange and yellow; the clean, freshness of it magnifying her need for a bath. After a struggling minute getting her oversized arm out of the way, she grabbed a clean set of clothes and crept down the hall. A heavy rustle of footsteps and chink of glass in the kitchen hastened her steps into the bathroom. She hooked the lock firmly and wiggled her gown over her head helping it over the curve of her cast. While the tub was filling, she discovered a small bottle of Ivory dishwashing liquid on the shelf above the sink and shot a stream of it into the hard spray of water until the foam of bubbles called her to take the plunge. To die and go to Heaven must be similar, she decided, wishing she could soak the stiffness of the white plaster that was propped a little too painfully on the rim of the tub.

"Toni?" The door knob turned but the hook latch held.

What nerve! "I'm here. I'll only be a minute," she replied.

"Do you need any help?"

"No thanks, I...oh!" She squawked, when her cast slipped almost reaching the water beneath the fluffy suds.

"Toni, open this door. What's going on in there?"

She could barely hear him above the racket he made jerking back and forth on the door. She had no idea why, but something about the whole scene struck her funny bone and she laughed until her side ached.

"Toni! Open the door." He shouted.

"I c...can't." She giggled. She laughed harder, but didn't know why. Her arm was killing her.

She heard a booming "hell fire" before his steps moved away. About the time she regained control the footsteps returned along with a long silver blade that gleamed in the crack of the door. One quick jerk upwards and the door flew wide open. Toni caught her shocked breath at the sight of Judd's furious face and slid lower into the water, but the tub bottom was soapy and she kept sliding.

"Oh...Judd!"

Alarmed, she clutched at the reaching arms as his fingers dug into her foam covered shoulders bringing her to a stable sitting position. Her good arm that had wrapped itself across her bare breasts was not good enough and her anger at the daring intrusion belted through her as she sent a large spray of soapy water right into his face.

"Why you little witch." He wiped the water from his eyes and before she knew what was happening, he grasped her around the waist and lifted her nude body from the water, exposing her fully. His eyes raked her shamelessly and what Toni saw in that face made her gasp in alarming intrigue of what she knew was inevitable.

"Judd." She closed her eyes, mortified.

"Open your eyes, Toni. You're not a child. You're a woman with a body like I had never imagined. You're beautiful."

She couldn't look at him but trembled helplessly. A warm hand caressed her face; her lower body pulled slowly against the rough material of his jeans. "Please, no." Her mind rebelled but her body was surging with responses quickly going beyond her control when his caresses reached the soapy tips of her breasts. A gentle tug on her hair brought her face up and his wet lips moistened hers before taking full possession of her mouth. No girlhood fantasy of what it felt like to be touched this way by a man had prepared her for this. Rationalization was distorted.

"What have I been doing? You could never be like her," he moaned.

Sobriety returned with force, changing response to a gut-wrenching hurt making her suddenly feel a lewd, self-disgust. She stiffened against his embrace and he suddenly stepped back, his blue eyes squinting with worry.

"Did I hurt you? Toni?"

"Yes, yes, my arm. Please hand me a towel." Her throat filled, escaped tears stinging bitterly. She wanted to scream, to flail him with her fist, but first she wanted her clothes.

A sigh of relief fled her lips when he jerked a large towel from the rack behind him and draped her.

0   "I'm sorry, Toni. I didn't think. Are you all right?" Genuine concern was evident, but it didn't lessen the real pain inside her.

"Just let me dress and I'll rest awhile."

Toni held her breath as he scanned her face searchingly before finally going out, watching the floor as he walked.

She hurried as much as possible with a useless arm into jeans and a sleeveless T-shirt.

Steam from a breakfast tray beside her bed mixed with the smoke from Judd's freshly ground out cigarette when she entered her room. He sat bent forward in a chair, elbows resting on either knee. His gaze held hers almost trance-like and she despised the weakening in her knees. His denim shirt sleeves were wet and clumps of suds still lingered on his jeans' legs.

"I'm sorry." He said quietly.

For what! Spilling your guts over a lost love. Letting me know I can't measure up. Her brain told her to scream the words at him, but she just nodded an acceptance.

"It's better now. Food smells good." She lied, setting on the edge of the bed managing a bite of toast.

"You must be telling the truth. An appetite's a good sign.

"Maybe you should try the same."

"No thanks. I ate with the chickens...well, *somebody's* chickens this morning.

"I mean the part about telling the truth." She wished too late she'd let that line go down with the toast when his features sharpened suddenly.

"What do you mean by that?" He said brusquely.

"I mean, why did you marry me? The real reason?" She braced herself for anything except the crinkled grin that slowly spread his face.

"Ok. The real reason. Because I'm a man of my word. I distinctly remember promising to marry a young pigtailed little flirt some years ago. And I also remember a certain look she gave me. A dare is what it was. I've got a weakness for dares. I also believe a man is only as good as his word. I had no choice."

Toni stared in astonishment. "You remember that?"

"One of my worst habits. I have trouble forgetting, especially things I should."

"Like her?" She made a mental note to work on her *blurting*.

"*Now* what are you talking about?"

Toni knew from the frown that immediately lined his features that she had struck a nerve, but some protective instinct told her not to push.

In an effort to bring back a casual tone to the conversation, Toni said, "Oh, we've all loved and lost at one time or another. I was just wondering out loud what the women in your life were like. But I don't suppose that's my business. Our marriage is only a pretense for a short time, so I guess we're not obligated to be open and honest with each other. Right?"

He didn't answer and she nervously sipped her cooling coffee, sick with misery. There was a blank puzzlement in the face that stared at her. She wasn't all together sure she was glad she'd stopped him from making love to her, from letting him discover that she was a virgin. The thought sent a strong aching awareness of how close she'd come to being in Cowboy's bed right now, wrapped in his arms and made totally his wife. But it had to be right between them first. She wanted his love, not just out of an occasional need for a woman as he'd suggested last night, but because his love for her was solid and unpretentious.

"Get some rest," was all he offered before walking out.

She sighed. For all that had passed between Judd and herself the past few days, there seemed to be nothing between them at all. But there will be, she stubbornly convinced herself. You, Judd Luke, will love me like you've never loved a woman in your life. You can bet your fancy Stetson on it.

The remainder of the day, she slept fitfully, blaming her depressive tears on her physical weakness. She awoke late that evening to find a supper tray beside her bed and the following morning, a strong smell of coffee and scrambled eggs woke her in unison with the thud of a door closing. It was just as well that he kept his distance, she decided, at least until she was no longer such a burden.

Her appetite was surprisingly raging and after swallowing the last bite of her breakfast, a trouble free bath and fresh clothes made her feel as good as new. A light touch of makeup cheered her pale cheeks and after running a brush through her hair, she carried her food tray to the kitchen.

Her eyes swept the circumference of the kitchen from where she stood in the doorway. "Oh scream," she muttered. Dirty dishes were piled everywhere. Food and grease splatters covered the stove and cabinet.

Suddenly her eyes flickered with thought and a slow smile played at her lips. What better way does a woman have to a man's heart than to prove herself strong and capable in carrying her end of the load?

The task of washing dishes proved much more tedious than she had expected, but once done, she gave herself a verbal pat on the back and collapsed on the den couch. Stretching her arm and legs out to relieve the cramped muscles, she began to feel a disgust at the confining plaster on her fractured arm.

The awesome vastness of the Wyoming ranchland beckoned to her from outside the den window. The sun was high above the distant mountain peaks seeming to lay some sort of accepted claim to these few acres of the world. Toni felt a ridiculous twinge of envy that her presence wasn't half as welcomed. Time, she reminded herself. Give him time.

It was two o'clock when she slid a roast into the oven and set the timer for five thirty. She was startled at how quickly time passed when the buzzer sounded. She pulled the last couple pairs of jeans from the clothes dryer taking almost ten minutes to hang them straight. By six thirty she stood back to admire the table she'd managed to set and willed away the fatigue beginning to threaten her.

Quickly, she went to her room and slipped into a hot pink sundress and white flip flops. She brushed the sides of her hair away from her face, proud at how adept she was becoming as a one arm do-it-yourselfer. A little eye shadow brought her large eyes to life and a pink blusher on her cheeks completed the transformation. Satisfied with the casual sophistication reflected in her mirror, she headed back to the kitchen to make sure everything was perfect.

It was as perfect as she could have done with two arms, but moments later when Judd slammed noisily through the rear door and stopped at the kitchen entrance, Toni felt herself shrink at the condemnation in the man's eyes as they slowly moved from her surprise dinner to survey her slowly from head to toe. But she relaxed when he suddenly grinned, eyes dancing.

"Well, if this isn't a picture of home sweet home. Don't suppose there's any need to ask how you're feeling."

"I'm almost as good as new. I wasn't sure what time you'd be back. Guess my timing's not bad, huh."

Actually, Toni's heart was turning flips at her obvious success in pleasing her husband.

Judd removed his hat and scratched his head, sheepishly hesitant to come in. "Guess maybe I ought to clean up."

Toni suddenly wanted to run to him and throw herself into his arms, but moved instead toward the table to pour tea. "There's no need. Everything's ready."

Judd joined her at the table after washing his hands in the kitchen sink. Without a word, he sliced the roast cutting a portion into bite size pieces for her. Only casual conversation was exchanged during the course of the meal and had company been present, no one would have suspected that the situation between herself and Judd was anything less than newlywed bliss.

Finally, he pushed his empty plate away and sat tall in the straight backed chair, thumbs hooked in the edge of his jeans' pockets.

"Finest meal I've had in years, Mrs. Luke."

"Thank you."

"Must have been quite a task to clean up the mess I left and then cook a feast, all at the same time with one arm tied in a knot."

Toni smiled. "Well, I had all day to do it. I mean, I needed something to do to pass the hours. I'm glad you enjoyed it."

He lit a cigarette, never taking his eyes from her. "Did I tell you how pretty you look tonight?"

A mischievous smirk was suddenly all over his face and she nervously stood up gathering the dirty dishes. Things seemed to be moving too fast. "No, you didn't, but thanks. There's nothing like cleaning up a little after wallowing in a sick bed."

She caught the white of his smile from the corner of her eye and felt a tinge of panic rise inside her. She hadn't expected to do such a top notch job so quickly.

-336 A deeply tanned hand reached for her arm, forcing the dishes back onto the table. "Why don't you serve dessert? I'll handle the dishes for you later."

"D-dessert? I completely forgot about making dessert." She was almost proud there was a flaw in her grand display of wifeliness.

"No, you didn't." His grip tightened and he stood up towering above her, smashing his cigarette in the dinner plate. "You played the part of the little wife to perfection today. You cleaned our house, cooked us a fine supper, hung our clean wash noticeably on the laundry rack. And look at you. Not a hair out of place, dressed in a sexy little dress that a man wouldn't have to wrestle to get you out of. You've had dessert on your mind all day it seems."

"Judd!" She jerked her arm free, but in the same instant, he scooped her up in his arms pinning her only good one against his rock hard chest. Her protests were ignored as he carried her effortlessly into his own bedroom, letting her feet drop to the carpeted floor.

She stood as though welded to the spot staring with a heart pounding fear and anticipation of the wild passion smoldering in her husband's eyes.

Her mind was spinning frantically. 'You asked for this,' it taunted her. 'It's what you wanted. The man is your husband. You'll be his in the most intimate sense. But it's *not* right,' she fought with herself. 'He wants to punish me, to scare me. He doesn't love me.'

"Judd," she whispered a plea for some sort of understanding, but it went unheeded as she was pulled against the hard, muscled shape of his chest. His blue eyes danced like firelight upon his face, his breath, hot and damp, searing her blood rushed cheeks. She closed her eyes against the slow deliberate decent of his lips toward hers, anticipating, wanting, and desperately trying to find a way to prevent losing that special undefiled union with the man she loved to a few minutes of a meaningless romp.

But his lips never touched her and when the pressure of his embrace loosened, she opened her eyes to a mocking cold stare that cut through to her soul.

He released her and stepped back an arm's length. "I've got to hand it to you, my lady. You nearly pulled it off, right down to the last nickel. A consummated marriage could make for a better settlement."

She felt the blood drain from her face, shocked speechless for a moment. As the impact of what he meant settled on her, she began to tremble, her blood turning to ice.

"That's a lie," she choked out in a whisper.

"Really? This whole cozy little scene was a setup for a big dumb cowboy who was a sure fire target for a trip to the cleaners. You have nothing to lose, except *maybe* your virginity, and everything beyond that, pure profit."

"You...you're out of your mind. Have you forgotten who's responsible for this *cozy little set up?* I never wanted anything from you. But it's not hard to see through your sick reasoning. Anyone would have served your purpose. I just happened to come along at the right time. Lucky me!" Tears were threatening and she shook her head in an effort to stave them off.

"What are you getting at?"

"The female sex! You despise it enough to just pluck one off the street to see how much pain you can inflict on her. You've been burned by a woman, pretty bad, I'd say, and you're so ate up with it that anyone of the same gender would serve to ease your lust for revenge. That's the real reason you insisted on this...this...*marriage,* isn't it! Isn't it!" Even as hot tears blinded her to the white drawn features that plainly said that her Cowboy had been hurt beyond endurance, his silence was enough.

By the time she cleared the stinging blur from her eyes, Judd's back was to her. There was nothing more to say and nothing she could do to ease the crushing pain of knowing the love of her life had already given his heart away.

It was a moment before she could convince her shaky legs to take her out. She had pushed the truth at him in her anger and all that was left was suffering...his, for a woman who must have been the one love of his life; hers, for the love of her Cowboy who had none left to give.

"Toni." Judd's deep throated tone stopped her at the door. "If you have any ideas about leaving, forget it. Nobody would hire you with a broken arm." He turned a strained, rather bewildered face toward her and opened his mouth to speak, but closed it again. A silent nod toward the door dismissed her and without hesitation she turned and walked briskly to her room and leaned against the closed door just seconds before the dam broke. She hadn't cried like that in years and when she was finally under control again, she discovered that the painful blow her heart had taken only minutes ago had smoothed over somewhat, leaving a protective denial that she had ever really loved this cowboy. But it was only a numbness that soon replaced itself with a bewildering misery.

***

CHAPTER SIX

Long warm days drifted by. Toni stayed as busy as possible, sometimes dusting needlessly. The harder she worked, the less time she had to think about Judd.

One evening she wrote a short *all is well* note to Julie, not daring to mention her marriage or true state of affairs. In fact, the note was a lie, but wasn't that what her life was now. She had honored God the best she knew how. She believed He had given her an open door, even compelled her to use the last of her money and close out her life in Texas and head for Wyoming. All it brought her was heartache. Her muscles tightened against the surge of anger that rose up in her. Anger at God. Hot tears trickled from the corners of her eyes. *I'm sorry, Lord Jesus. I know you're still in control. I just don't get it.*

Up to now, she had managed to cope with the tension wrought by her circumstances, but even the strongest character could be broken and Toni was beginning to feel a definite crack. The feeling of expectancy, of breaking through the shield Judd had built around himself was giving way to hopelessness. His crumpled bed sheets were the only sign of his existence the past few days until today. He didn't come home at all.

Before addressing an envelope, it crossed her mind that maybe she should level with Julie and work out some arrangement to escape this heart crushing predicament. Perhaps she could obtain a loan from Julie's parents. She shuddered at the thought of having to unload the disastrous results of this stunt on them, but her desperation overruled.

She tossed the cheerful lies into the trash can and it was almost midnight when she signed *Toni Luke* at the bottom of the last page of a long letter. Her eyelids were heavy. Her heart and mind emotionally zapped. Rising from Judd's leather desk chair, she decided to prepare the letter for mailing after she relaxed in a hot bath.

Every bit of her confidence seemed to have deserted her. How she ever thought she could have achieved a beautiful end to such a hopeless beginning was beyond her. Living under false pretenses the past weeks had weakened her integrity, her openness. She hated every aspect of her existence. She would mail the letter and pray for the right results.

In a few minutes she eased down carefully into a tub of very warm water and felt good about her confessions to Julie, especially the painful truth that she was truly in love with her husband. She had desperately needed to verbalize the truth, even if it was only to one who could do nothing but listen.

The thought of leaving this ranch, leaving Cowboy, created a wildness of confusion inside of her. *I can't stay. I can't stay.* She knew she had to face facts; look at the truth and walk that direction. Nothing on the inside of her was peaceful with that decision, but she refused to live another day just breathing in lies and exhaling a sham. She had to mail the letter to Julie and get out while she had a shred of willpower left to go on.

Half an hour later, Toni returned to Judd's office clad only in her ever present arm cast and a knee length sleeveless cotton night shirt. She didn't remember closing the door and when she pushed it open, her blood ran cold at the sight of Judd sitting at his desk, the letter to Julie in his hand.

He looked up at her, wide eyes seeming to penetrate her own. There was no anger in them, but a strange wondering expression. A pulse throbbed painfully in her neck as she stood there anticipating a reaction. She had no idea how much he'd read.

It was Toni who finally broke the tense silence. "I believe that belongs to me," she said softly.

"No, it doesn't. This doesn't belong to anyone."

In a few seconds the letter lay in a crumpled ball in the trash on top of the first one.

"You had no right to do that." She snapped.

"Your problems are not the responsibility of a pal in Texas. You are *my* wife and *my* responsibility," he spoke with authority.

Toni opened her mouth to let fly with a nasty reply to the absurdity of his remark, but hesitated at the soft sincerity in his face. She stood frozen to the spot when he got to his feet and came slowly toward her, stopping a couple of steps from her. He was freshly shaven and wearing clean jeans and a crisp blue plaid shirt. His hair smelled like a sweet shampoo and she wondered where he had cleaned up. Her heart flipped over and she was unable to move her eyes away from the polished sapphires gleaming down at her.

"The letter, Toni. Was it the truth?"

She couldn't breathe properly at the moment, let alone remember all she had written in the letter. But she did know that she had poured out her heart to Julie. She had told her the total truth about everything that had happened since she arrived here.

"Yes," she finally managed.

Her heart jerked when he reached across the few feet separating them and pulled her by the front of her shirt until she felt his hot breath on her face.

"Then say it to me. Tell me to my face what you told your friend, Julie."

"What do you want me to say?"

"That you love me." His touch scorched the sides of her neck as he held her face upwards.

For a long time she said nothing, but stared with a soft, radiant, glowing face. Her heart felt as though it had melted and smeared all over her insides in answer to the loving tenderness in his eyes. Finally she found her voice.

"It's true, Cowboy." Tears were brimming in her eyes now, but she didn't care. "I love you. I *way* love you."

Judd stood silent, his emotions flickering and shimmering across his gorgeous face. He saw love in her eyes, a love he wanted only from her, a love he could believe in and trust. He felt a desperation rise up inside him. This woman, his wife, had just laid her heart bare in the words he'd read in the letter. And now, the truth was glittering like tiny diamonds in her eyes. He could see her love, feel it, taste it in the inches of space that separated their bodies. And, God help him, his heart just openly fell at her feet. That same heart he had vowed to never let out of his control just stripped its gears. And right this minute, he didn't care.

The sound of *way love you,* penetrated his entire being. He wanted to say something, to convey the emotional wash of desire, his desperate need of her. But he couldn't speak past the lump in his throat. He'd have to show her. His thumb tenderly stroked her cheek. He couldn't tear his eyes from hers. His lips came down slow, sensual, then eagerly claimed hers in a kiss that she returned without inhibition. Her free arm found it's way around his neck as his hands caressed her possessively. He stroked her hair, rubbed her back, and chose, then and there, to trust, to love, to believe.

"Toni," he groaned against her mouth. "I love you. I always did. Even long ago."

Toni pulled back slightly dizzy with joy and confusion. "Long ago? When was long ago?"

Judd planted a wet kiss on her lips and smiled. "When I was on the verge of committing a terrible sin. Why do you think I just up and left John Baxter's ranch?"

She stared at him trying to grasp what he was saying.

"I fell in love with a fourteen year old child. Good old Uncle John saw the signs and fired me. I didn't blame him. I needed my butt whipped You had no idea what that kind of love was about. You were a baby."

Toni chuckled through her surprise. "A baby? Babies don't hide in the hay barn crying with a broken heart the way I did the day you left."

It was his turn to look surprised then and Toni smiled lovingly up at the blue twinkles shining brighter than she'd ever seen them. Yet, behind those twinkles, she knew there was still a private battle raging, and she knew it would surface again. But it wasn't there now. *Now* there was nothing but a powerful and overwhelming love that filled Toni, heart and soul.

He hesitated a few seconds, then gently touched a warm calloused hand to her cheek. "I want you to be my wife. Does that scare you?"

Toni closed her eyes and took a deep breath. He wanted to make love to her and it did frighten her, but only because she couldn't get rid of the doubts hounding her. There were things she had to understand first.

Toni reached and covered the hand now caressing her neck and looked at him with eyes huge and vulnerable. Judd..."

"I won't hurt you, baby," he told her.

She shook her head. "I know that."

"Then what is it?"

She hesitated, choosing her words, knowing she might open a wound that could destroy this moment.

He smiled at her in a way that almost convinced her to let it alone, but she couldn't.

"I just don't understand your sudden change of heart."

"It's not a sudden change. There's nothing to understand except that I love you and want you to stay with me. I want you to become mine completely." The sincerity in his eyes should have been enough to convince her, but she couldn't seem to brush aside the memory of the overwhelming bitterness she had seen before.

"Judd, I want that too, more than you know. But we have to talk first. I have to know that...that..."

"That I'm not trying to take you to bed just because I can?" His hands dropped to his sides and he turned, putting a few steps between them. When he turned again to face her, lines of strain were etched around his eyes and Toni's heart went out to him. He spoke slowly, choosing his words.

"Julie Langston's father was a friend of my father's. The ad that was sent to Langston was a set-up deal for me and for you."

"Me?" Toni felt her mouth freeze open and her mind jerked backward momentarily to the strange conversation she'd had with Mr. Langston about the ad.

"Dad made a deal with him to use that as a means to entice you here in hopes of kindling a fire in me to marry."

"But why? And why me?"

"Dad knew why your uncle fired me and I only suppose through correspondence with Langston he learned about your friendship with Julie and the fact that you were sort of foot loose."

Toni stared at him, a pulse throbbing behind her saucer eyes. "I don't understand this, Judd. Why...why was he so anxious for you to marry that he would devise such a scheme?"

It only lasted a second, but Toni saw that far off look flicker in his eyes again like a memory haunting him.

"The reason doesn't matter. It's history."

There was a moment of silence during which Toni decided it best to leave that part alone, for now.

"How did you find this out?" she asked finally

"Sky told me about it just tonight. He opened my eyes to a lot of things."

"Where does Sky fit into all this?"

"Sky Cooper ranched with my father for years, long before Dad acquired this place and hired him as foreman. Dad told Sky about his plans but he didn't believe he'd actually pull such a stunt. At least not until you showed up."

Suddenly he grinned, shaking his head. "It really is a shame he didn't have a chance to see his little plan work so perfectly."

"Has it worked so perfectly?"

She was drawn carefully back into his warm muscular arms. "I love you. And you love me. I'd call that perfect."

"Cowboy," she breathed tremulously and welcomed his kiss. All caution concerning the strange unanswered 'history' was lost in the heated pulsating desire coursing through her being.

Minutes later, breathless, "I want you in my bed tonight where you belong, Toni, and every night from now on." She felt his hands hot against her skin where he had pushed her night shirt off of her shoulders. His lips burned a trail of fire across her heaving chest, then teased her into an urgency of passion that almost made her crazy. He swung her body up in his arms and carried her into his bedroom, and kicked the door shut behind them. He laid her gently on top of the quilted bed comforter mindful of the now intolerable arm cast. She reached to turn out the bedside lamp, but he caught her hand and stretched her arm above her head. Without a word, he began unfastening the remaining buttons of her shirt and worked the sleeve over her cast, keeping his eyes locked on hers. He dropped the shirt behind him to the floor. As she lay on his bed, totally naked, it was a long minute before Judd could satisfy his need to just look at her. Beautiful. He had never seen anything to compare with the beauty of her body. Whatever passion he'd felt for any woman before this moment was forgettable. This went far past a physical attraction, but he couldn't define the contentment that sweetened his insides. Like he was...home, after a long exile. If by some horrible event, he was only standing here dreaming her, *let me never wake up.*

Their eyes continued to drink from each other's while he removed his clothes, then he stretched out beside her.

"Cowboy?" she whispered, feeling a slight panic rise in her.

"I know, baby girl," he whispered. What he knew was, he was about to take her virginity and as much as he wanted to fulfill his promise of not hurting her, he probably was going to. And for all his efforts to prepare her fully, to wait for her, to arouse her to be ready for him to take her virgin body, he hoped he was ready himself.

He took her as gently and quickly as possible, but the unexpected rip of pain brought a moaning scream out of her. In the same instant, Judd let out a howl of pain when he felt the razor sharp fingernails gouging his back. After a moment, he rested his forehead on hers and started to laugh. "If I didn't know better, I'd swear you planned that."

He raised his head and looked at her, realizing she didn't even know what she'd done to him. Her cheeks were wet, her eyes closed.

"Open your eyes, sweetheart."

She looked at him, then and it dawned on him for the first time just how naïve and unassuming his young bride really was. How had he been so lucky to have this unspoiled, innocent young virgin show up at his door and step into his carefully guarded heart? And she had just given him, *Judd Luke*, the one part of her she'd obviously kept in reserve for that one special man. Who was *he* to have been so willingly, eagerly given her gift?

Her eyes were pooled with a mixture of pain and desire, invoking an involuntary tightening in his stomach, partly from regret that he'd just hurt her, and partly from the forced restraint of his own raging lust.

"I'm sorry." He kissed the tears on both of her cheeks. "You didn't know that had to happen, did you?"

"I didn't know...it would hurt *that* bad." She blinked quickly and willed the remainder of her tears away. "What did you think I planned?"

"Didn't you hear me squeal like a little girl? You ripped my back open with your finger nails, you animal," he laughed.

She smiled then. "Much as I'd like to, I just can't find it in me to feel sorry about that."

"Oh so that's how you are, huh?" He pretended to cop an attitude. "I'll show you sorry." He reached out and turned off the lamp.

It was real. It wasn't just a beautiful dream that passed with the night. Cowboy was beside her, his eyes proving his love all over again when she opened her eyes and found him propped on an elbow smiling down at her.

"What a woman!" he said, then whistled softly through his teeth.

The dreamy course sound of his voice seemed to hang in the air around her and Toni reached to pull his lips to hers.

"You're mine, Toni Luke," he said after a long moment. "Say it."

The urgency in his tone squeezed her heart and she longed to ask about his uncertainties. But not now, she told herself. Nothing was as important as this beautiful moment.

"Yes, Judd Cowboy Luke, I'm yours. Never doubt that."

Slowly he drew back the covers exposing every inch of her. His hands explored her body while he kissed her with renewed passion, then suddenly sat up and slapped her thigh sharply.

"Get up, woman."

"Not yet. Later." She reached for him again but he laughed and playfully pushed her arm away.

"Do as you're told before I have to prove who wears the pants in this house." He helped her to a sitting position, grinning broadly as he watched her shaking with laughter. "What's so funny?"

"What pants? Where?"

He laughed as he got up and began dressing. "You have a point there, lady.

"Okay, so what does the tyrannical lord and master want for breakfast," she asked as she worked her cast into a sleeve of her night shirt.

"Nothing."

"Nothing?"

"How about a picnic lunch later? Pack a couple of sandwiches and get your boots on. We're going for a ride."

She pinched herself to be sure she was awake while she knocked herself out getting to her room. Her room? A shiver of warm joy shot through her.

A half hour later, she stood in the back yard, brown bag in hand, waiting for Judd. A gentle breeze caressed her deliriously happy face and she hadn't given a thought to her bum arm until Judd emerged from the barn leading one horse. Of course he wouldn't let her on a mount of her own yet. He helped her into the saddle along with the sack lunch before swinging himself up behind her. One strong sun-browned arm held her tightly around the waist making her tremble at the confident power in it. His other hand expertly reined the horse toward the open field.

"Where are we going?" she inquired over her shoulder, not really caring.

"To our secret honeymoon hideaway," he growled into her ear just before kicking the big gelding into a fast lope through the open gate and across the wide grassland.

Toni laid her head against Judd's wide chest, relishing the cool wind on her burning skin. If this was a dream, she prayed she would never, never wake up.

Before long, the pasture land changed into a sparse forest of pine trees that gradually grew thicker. The Christmassy scent invigorated her already well awakened senses.

Judd reined the horse into a walk as they made their way down a steep embankment that leveled out into a shallow creek. He stopped in the center of it to allow the horse to drink.

Toni had been lost in thought during most of the ride. She remembered over and over the earnestness in Judd's ruggedly handsome face when he first admitted that he loved her. And she tried, with sufficient success to block out the flashes of intuition that all was not as well as it seemed.

Neither of the riders spoke, but sat silently astride the thirsty animal, savoring the peace and beauty of the countryside.

Toni's eyes studied the image laying darkly on the opposite bank a man, tall and lean with tendrils of hair etched below a wide brimmed hat. Her own shadow was cast in front of his, the pair seeming to melt into the other then, as she felt Judd's cool wet lips against her neck.

There was something about being out in the wild, open country alone with a man of Judd's caliber...capable, forceful and openly wanting that brought out the primitive in her. She was trembling and wondered if the dull needing ache in her loins was natural for a woman to feel. But, Judd was her husband and when she felt both of his hands caressing her breasts suddenly, she really didn't care what the answer was.

"Toni," she heard him groan against her wind tangled curls. Then he reached for the reins dangling high on the horse's neck and kicked him into a fast move down the middle of the creek, then up onto the bank. He dismounted, then lifted her down before tying the horse a few feet away.

Toni looked around frowning at the odd feeling that something was missing. Then she saw it and covered her eyes in exasperation at the sight. Realizing what had probably caused it made her laugh.

"*Now* what's so funny," Judd asked as he came to stand beside her.

She pointed and he looked down the creek a few yards at the brown paper bag bobbing up and down, its contents washed part of the way out. When he turned back to her, a disgusted smirk wrinkled his mouth, but his eyes were laughing.

"You're going to pay dearly for that, woman. My torture chamber is just around the bend. Come on." He caught her wrist and pulled her laughing behind him along the creek bank until they rounded a corner.

The scenery changed right before her eyes and she knew Judd was pleased by her stunned reaction. Thick tufts of green grass spread like a blanket beneath a nearly perfect circle of huge pines with several odd willowy branches forming a shelter above it. A cluster of rocks made a jagged step-down into a deep pool of greenish blue water. A small rocky crevice in the far end of the pool created a trickling waterfall that added the finishing touch to a virtual Garden of Eden.

She drew in her breath, incredulously. "It's beautiful. Cowboy, it's..."

Before she could finish, his lips found hers. There was no more talk for a long time. Judd swept her up in his arms and carried her across the threshold of their honey moon hide-a-way and lay her upon nature's cool green blanket.

"Now you pay," he whispered.

**

CHAPTER SEVEN

The green canopy of pine trees created an illusion of privacy making the fact that Judd was slowly and mercilessly relieving her of every thread of clothes she had just put on, seem safe and comfortable.

Laying strip stark naked under the deeply shaded morning sun brought out a primitive yeehaw cowgirl she didn't know was there. She was sure every woman in America, young and old, would be seething with jealousy if they could just see her now.

The now nude form of her Cowboy husband stood over her grinning like a cat with feathers in its mouth. She tried to steady her gaze on his face, to hold a longing *I want you* look that would not give away what she was really thinking. She tried hard, but it wasn't happening. Hilarious laughter burst out of her like a water hose turned on full throttle. Partly because this *mostly* naked god-like specimen of a man standing over her, attempting to aim some authoritative weight down on her, was wearing nothing but his boots and spurs, his fruit of the looms wrapped around one boot. She was sure she had just watched him lose the boots before tugging off his jeans. The other part was the realization that Cowboy was still *anything for a laugh* Cowboy in full goofy bloom.

That revelation peering down at her changed her raucous, side splitting laughter into tears. Now she was literally crying. They were tears of joy, riding the edge of hysteria.

Whether he fully got it or not, Cowboy dropped down beside her and wrapped her up in his arms, a protective leg thrown across hers.

"It's okay, sweet girl," he whispered into her hair. "I know I'm an ass. At least I can still make you laugh."

Suddenly she was laughing again, cackling like a hen, then dissolved into more tears. She couldn't get a grip.

When her emotions finally spun out, she realized Judd had a near death grip on her, holding her without questions, without needing an explanation. He just held her, resting with her for a few silent minutes at the end of it. Except for his nearly suffocating grip, she would have thought he'd fallen asleep.

"Judd?"

"What, baby?"

"I have to pee."

Without moving, he muttered, "Pick a tree, get on the outside and squat."

"That's gross." She giggled and squirmed to break free of his hold. "Don't look."

He raised up on his elbow and raked her up and down with his eyes, raising his eyebrows in mock surprise. "You mean I haven't seen it all? There's more?" He laughed and slapped a hand over his eyes. "Hurry up. You've got one minute, then I'm looking."

Judd rested his head on his arm, willing his eyes into submission. That protective instinct was shouting at him to keep one eye on her, she's out in the wide open range buck naked, but he knew the hands were a couple miles the other side of the creek today. He shot a glance at the pile of clothes close by and smiled. Put it on simmer, boy, he chided himself. She's not going anywhere.

With a jerk, he realized it had been nearly five minutes since Toni had left. He jumped to his feet, forgetting he still wore boots and one boot still wore his underwear. The spur on his opposite boot grabbed the material and when he took a step, he splattered face down, spurs locked up behind him.

"Hell's bells," he mumbled into the grass.

Before he could collect himself, a squeal of laughter rang in his ears from the opposite side of the hideaway. He jerked his head up and saw Toni's head floating in the middle of the pool, her mouth stretched from ear to ear in pure delirious laughter.

"I'm all right." he managed to grate between his teeth. "Don't be concerned."

The head sticking out of the water bobbed up and down, laughing harder.

"I'm fine, really." he hissed, then through his tight lips, *just let me get my hands around those tonsils!*

Finally after rolling and flipping a few times, Judd emerged barefoot, and in two strides and one flying leap, he landed feet first almost on top of her in the water hole. His first thought was to duck her under the water, but the second thought took priority.

"Toni, your cast!"

"Oh!" She lifted her arm up, feeling the extra water soaked weight. She stared at her arm then looked up to meet the concern in his eyes. A mischievous smile squinted up at him.

"Too late now," she said matter of fact. "We'll deal with that later." She pressed her body against him and wrapped her good arm around his neck, pushing herself up on tiptoes to tease the half smile on his lips as she spoke.

"Right now," she cooed, "we have some serious honey-mooning going on."

Standing a little over waist deep in the creek hole, Judd battled momentarily with what needed attention first. Her arm? Her sudden volcanic need to be touched, loved by him?

Inner delight rippled through him as he shot fiery sapphire sparks down into those *I want you* rounded brown eyes. His answer was none too gentle as his arm came around her beneath the water and pulled her tighter against him, his mouth matching the crushing demands of hers.

Toni felt all reason and sanity explode into bits inside her, leaving a wanton need for her man...her Cowboy to know again the secrets of her body. She was definitely liking the freedom of her soul that was found inside of this institution of marriage. The freedom to be who she was inside was priceless.

And to be able to give it all to the one man in the world who she wanted to be with and then see and feel him receive it from her and give back to her with the same open intensity...all at once. If there were no other clues to be had that alone was enough to know her God was real.

Judd slid an arm slowly down her backside, then lifted her into his arms.

Toni watched, without shame, as his eyes swept over her naked flesh. He was enjoying his *husband's* privilege as much as she reveled in viewing his open desire.

He carried her to the edge of the pool in the middle of the gentle waterfall and laid her on a smooth flat slab of rock that shimmered with a thin layer of running water. With the grace of a majestic mountain cat, he lifted himself out of the water and lowered his length on top of her.

It was the middle of the afternoon when the pair returned to the house. As soon as his horse was put up and fed, Judd drove Toni into town to re-do the soggy cast. Even though it was late after waiting hours for a doctor to get around to her, happiness and contentment could not be packaged any more glorious than the way it was draped over Judd and Toni Luke. They showered together, ate like they hadn't seen a biscuit in a week, and fell into bed and slept, arms and legs tangled...

Several weeks had passed since those first glorious hours of love Toni had experienced with her husband. Nothing had come to mar the loving atmosphere in the little frame ranch house on the Double OO as they settled into a comfortable routine.

She worked hard caring for their home, but now with a song in her soul. Judd came home each evening dusty and tired to a scrumptious meal and later to hours of talk and laughter and love making.

A thought occurred to Toni one evening while making Judd his favorite supper of hot dogs and sauerkraut that it would be a nice gesture to thank all the ranch hands for their extra hours in the saddle the night she was hurt and lost. She could cook for them. A smile creased her face imaging them sitting down to sauerkraut and dogs. No, she'd do much better than that.

Judd mulled over her idea that night as he polished off his supper.

"Good idea. Nothing a working cowboy likes better than food." He cocked one eye up at her and grinned as she cleared the table. "Well, almost nothing better."

She stared at him blankly for a moment before his insinuation registered. She tightly wrung the dish towel in her good hand and let the end of it fly, landing a sharp pop on his shoulder.

He laughed and quicker than the eye grabbed the end of the retreating towel, pulling her to him. In one motion he slid his chair back, pulled her across his lap, careful with her bum arm, and playfully paddled her butt.

That squealing laughter filling the kitchen was what he lived for. Toni was happy. Happy with him. What more could a man want in this world besides a frisky little cowgirl for a wife and a plate of sauerkraut and dogs.

Judd gently grasped her upper arms and stood her back upright. "Wanna go for round two? Take another shot, little lady."

"Would you be serious for one minute," she scolded through her laughter.

His expression deadpanned. "Ok. I'm serious now."

"How about a cookout" T-bone steaks. "

"T-bones!" His eyes bugged out. "How bout I get some beer and you re-heat this left over kraut for them."

Her eyes rolled. "Is that all their hard riding was worth?" They found my poor battered body, for heaven sake and lost their shirts for their trouble. "

"Ok, ok. Steaks. "

"*T*-bone steaks." She popped him with the towel again.

"Yeah...round two!" He lurched toward her, missing a grasp on her as she fled toward the bedroom, giggling like a school girl. "You better run, woman," he yelled as he rushed in right on her heels and kicked the door shut behind them.

It was a perfect afternoon for steaks on the grill. A slight breeze, odd for windy Wyoming, kept the suns heat at bay. Sunday afternoon was Cowboy's idea so the guys could enjoy their beer and retire early to sleep it off. Drinking on the ranch was prohibited except for special gatherings like this and Judd couldn't remember another time like this.

All of the hands showed. Eight, not counting the hosts and including C.J., the chuck wagon cook. Judd endured the good natured teasing about the pink checkered apron Toni had tied around his middle after C.J. sneaked it over to her.

"I think Cook here's been holding out on us boys," Judd announced as he flopped the last sizzling T-bone on the huge platter. "Don't ya'll wonder what he's doing with a pink apron? I know my inquiring minds want to know."

All eyes shot to the cook with a few hoots and accusations, bringing a flush and a sheepish grin to the older man's face.

"Truth is, I cook better than I do laundry. That apron use to be red checkered."

"Sounds fishy to me," Les piped.

"Yeah, who you hidin' out with in that old cabin of yours?" Doyle pushed, grinning.

C.J. looked at the ground and kicked up the dirt with the toe of his boot. "I don't know about you boys, but there's one thing my mama taught me real early on and that's that you don't mess with your cook. Mess with the bull, but never the cook.

Laughter rang out around the yard as Judd waved his arm and yelled to come and get it.

In record time, the steaks were gone, along with large bowls of potato salad, red beans and yeast rolls. Toni was surprised to see the large sauerkraut platter empty. These men had to be tough hombres to eat that stuff. And after all that, the six chocolate pies, Toni's scratch specialty, were inhaled within minutes.

Judd had disappeared for a few minutes, then reappeared from around the side of the house carrying a medium sized box. A series of taps on his beer bottle got everyone's attention. "Gentlemen, I believe my wife has something she wants to say." He turned and winked, knowing he'd caught her off guard.

Without hesitation, Toni faced them and before she could utter one word, she felt a lump begin to form. She cleared her throat. "Well, I guess I'm going to be a cry bag about it, sorry. But this little dinner this afternoon was mine and Judd's way of trying to thank all of you for saving my life. This is hardly enough for all of your hours riding half the night..." Her voice cracked and she looked over at Judd. He instantly stepped to her side and set the box down, then draped an arm snuggly around Toni. "New Wrangler shirts. Everybody's size should be in there." He looked down at Toni and gave her a quick squeeze as she swiped an escaped tear from her cheek. "Thanks, boys. I personally owe you big time."

"Shoot, Toni," drawled A.J., "you could head for the hills at least once a week. We'd come hunt you up about noon and be here for T-bones that evening."

"Count me in," came a shout from across the yard.

"Me too," came another.

Judd jerked his apron off and threw it at the quickly retreating, lanky-legged instigator.

Toni giggled, shook her head and headed for the back door with a load of picnic stuff while Cowboy passed out shirts.

An hour later, Judd poured the last quarter of a bottle of beer into the wind dried grass beside the back steps. He leaned against the wooden railing and stared into the now empty silent dusk that enveloped the back yard. He couldn't remember ever feeling so contented with his life.

Only the fact that he had allowed Toni to believe his whole livelihood consisted of this working ranch and comfortable old farm house interrupted that contentment with a twinge of guilt. They had become a real couple. More than that, husband and wife with a growing bond of love and compatibility. It worried him that she might count the part of his life that he was keeping secret from her a breach of trust or respect.

Maybe in the beginning that was true. But she obviously wasn't looking for a money-bags sugar daddy. She was a meticulous little homemaker, a tiger in the sack and could get as dirt and poop covered as he could in a cow pen. And loved every minute of it. He grinned, then chuckled at the images his mind conjured up of her *cowboying* escapades around the barn. And despite the silly havoc of those times, she was a real good hand where it counted. It was almost other-worldly watching her calm a rank colt and he'd already decided he would need to brush up on his roping skills to stay up with her.

A million times now, he had thought about telling her that he didn't actually live here. In this house. But not yet. He didn't want their mundane riding, roping and loving life to change one iota. It was so perfect and simple. But eventually he would tell her the truth. Show her. And maybe the *grapevine*, such as it was, wouldn't spoil his plan for him before he was ready to show and tell.

The chinking of pots and pans drew his attention toward the back door. That was his wife in there, washing dishes after cooking for and serving his friends. How in the world did he attract such a beautiful lady, a lover, a cook and homemaker all wrapped up in one dynamite little package? Everything about her, without a word spoken, said *I love* you. She loved him.

He entered the kitchen and stopped when she looked up at him. The tender expression twinkling in her eyes held him more tightly than a physical touch. Judd wanted to move the few steps across the kitchen to touch her, but was held spellbound by the connection they were exchanging.

After a moment, she walked into Cowboy's arms and he held her, rocking her gently.

"Thank you, baby. You sure know how to throw a party."

"Oh, twernt nothing, mister", she cooed up at him with a mock -deep- south drawl.

"Yes, it was. It was something to me."

She was surprised at his serious tone.

"You've made a home for me. For us. That means more to me than you know."

He reached for her face and held it turned up to his. He'd never seen anything so beautiful. Never wanted anything as bad as he wanted this woman. *His woman. His wife.*

Blue sparkles glimmered in his eyes, passion fire shooting straight at her, filling every need she'd ever had. Her mom and dad. A sibling. A grandpa or grandma. The natural bonding of family relationships that she'd never experienced were not lost. Somehow, every thought or wonder or yearning dissolved as she remained still and drank in his love until her whole being trembled with pure joy.

This husband of hers could be the wackiest sky larker or the most thorough, passionate lover. But this was a new side. A raw opening of his soul's door was pulling her, begging her, imploring her heart to be one with his. This was a deeper need she was witnessing in her Cowboy than she understood. Was she enough to fill up that kind of need?

Lightly he brushed his lips against hers. So light, she was amazed at the feathery tenderness of his touch.

Then later in bed, as he watched the sweetness of peace, unadulterated contentment lighting her delicate face as she lay curled in the bend of his warm flesh, he wondered about her God. Oh, he certainly believed in God. But with Toni, there seemed to be something *more* than he knew anything about. Church attendance had never been a part of his experience. And she had never talked about going. But she talked about Jesus sometimes as though He was some special Friend of hers. He couldn't put his finger on it just yet, but somehow he felt deep inside himself that he was traveling toward something far bigger than life on the Double OO. He wasn't sure it was a good feeling.

Judd pulled Toni closer, wrapping his arms around her and pulled her almost beneath him as though to ensure she wouldn't disappear. And he thanked God.

With her arm mended, the warm sunny days drew Toni's thoughts toward the barn and arena, urging her to get back in the saddle again.

"After all," she proceeded one evening across the supper table when Judd showed no response at her excited chatter about riding again, "I could be of some help to you. Four hands are better than two, don't you think?"

Judd's reply was quiet and completely uncritical. A hint of laughter twinkled in his eyes. "Do I remember right...that you promised to love and obey me."

Toni's mouth opened to speak but confusion creased her brows and silenced a reply.

"Yes or no," he chuckled at her loss of words.

"Well, yes."

He reached across the table and squeezed her hand warmly. "And you have loved me like I never thought any woman could." The laughter in his eyes slowly faded. "But you will not do a man's work on this ranch. That includes risking your beautiful little neck on those colts."

Toni's heart sank. "That's not fair. You know I can ride *and* throw a rope. Anyway, where does it say it's strictly a man's world out there?" She sipped her iced tea trying to keep a matter-of-fact air about the conversation.

Judd pushed his plate aside and folded his long muscled arms along the edge of the table, expelling a sigh that brought Toni's eyes to meet his. His voice was strained when he finally spoke.

"Toni, one of the reasons that I love you is because of your love for the lifestyle I have here. It may well be the reason our marriage will succeed. We both almost have to be married to this land as equally as to each other. However, you are a woman. And more importantly, *my* woman, not my ranch hand. I won't allow you to work alongside the men I pay to do that work."

She blinked back the mist clouding her eyes. The protective strength which her husband inflicted into the words *my woman* caused a tingle to warm her body. It didn't matter that he had misunderstood her. Working like a paid cowhand was not what she meant. However, he had just admitted that her working alongside him, sharing his life's work was important and that's all she wanted.

Toni's heart thumped hard when Cowboy stood suddenly and grasped her upper arm and pulled her up into his arms. His sensuous, wanting smile met her own open invitation when she raised her face to his.

"You make me crazy, baby," he groaned, then crushed her mouth against his.

She clung to him, aching with desire.

"Pigtails. Tell me you love me," he mumbled against her lips.

The urgency in his voice was unmistakable; that need for reassurance. Toni was sure now that the underlying cause of Judd's doubts about her love for him was because of a deep rooted hurt inflicted by a woman. A woman he once loved deeply.

She placed her free hand on the side of his face and locked her gaze to his, willing him to see the love she felt for him as it poured up out of her heart. "I love you." She stressed the words slowly. "You're *my* Cowboy. *Mine.* Silently, she said *thank you* to the unknown woman who had given her the chance to show this big beautiful man what real love was about.

The next morning at breakfast, Judd told her, "I won't be back for supper. I have a meeting in Jackson. I'll be late so lock up and go on to bed."

"A meeting?" she asked surprised.

"Cut and dried business. When's the last check up on your arm due?"

Was he deliberately trying to change the subject?

"Day after tomorrow. What sort of meeting?"

The annoyed glance he shot at her was disturbing, to say the least, but his answer bristled her.

"Just personal business."

He stood and drained his coffee cup, then planted a light peck on her lips.

She heard him leave but she didn't look up. This wasn't his usual manner. Except for the quick kiss, he made her feel like the housekeeper again.

Well this is silly, she scolded herself silently. Judd is running a good sized operation out here and she simply hadn't had time to learn much about it. So what. I'll learn how it works all in good time.

Toni busied herself most of the day with small menial chores mainly to pass the time.

That evening, after a light supper, she retired to the study to bury herself in a good novel, a luxury she hadn't afforded herself since she'd been at the Double OO. Judd's office was definitely a man's idea of drab. He's probably never even noticed, she mused, and made a mental note to surprise him with a re-do someday.

His massive desk sat in the middle of the back half of the room, a new Apple computer perched on one end of it. A fax took up the small extension table right beside it. At least Judd kept in step with the latest equipment, even though a cell phone connection was hopeless.

Directly behind the desk several rows of various books, from Louis L 'Amour westerns to ranch management journals lined the small shelving unit against the wall...Rounding the corner of the desk, Toni noticed the sheet of paper on the fax that she didn't remember being there the day before. Mildly curious, she picked it up and realized it was a personal letter in a woman's handwriting. She felt herself tremble knowing before she began to read it, she was about to discover something she wasn't sure she wanted to know.

Her heart pounded as she backed up and sank into the desk chair. Quickly she skimmed the page. *Dearest Vinny, I can't tell you how excited I am to share your life in this way. You've made me so happy. Your phone calls are so special to me and am very glad to hear that you've taken a break from company travels. I look forward to our time together Thursday evening. My love, Maggie.*

The next few minutes were like a nightmare. She couldn't wake up. *Vinny?* A series of emotions, hurt, anger, confusion were all passing through her being at once. This was his business meeting. A woman named Maggie.

Toni wasn't sure how long she had sat there despising Judd Luke and allowing the power of her own stupidity to depress her, but she finally found the strength to put the letter back where she got it and walk on wooden legs to the kitchen. Suddenly panicked, she walked briskly out the back door into the cool night air. The moon gave enough light to mark her way to the barn where she plopped down on a hay bale.

"How could he!" she grated aloud. The memory of the night Judd had taken her virgin body into his bed, made her his wife in the fullest sense brought a moan of heartache to her lips in unison with an almost unbearable yearning to be held in his arms right now. The whole of her experience the past weeks had not been just blissfully, incredibly happy, but spiritually preordained as well. She knew it! Her life here was complete and solid and whoever this Maggie was could not possibly break that covenant. Could she?

Toni was deeply in love with her husband, with or without his horses. Or his ranch. Or the cowboy lifestyle that came with him. *Oh Jesus, this hurts so much.* She felt herself sinking into a dark hole.

Then as though she had been struck, she sat up straight and furiously swiped at an escaped tear. The thought of Judd touching another woman, making love to someone else filled her with rage, but tears had never solved a dilemma for her yet.

She was not a crybaby. She was a fighter. *He's mine and he's going to stay mine*!

She didn't have a single moment to plan her first course of action before the barn light snapped on and she found herself staring into the startled face of a young cowboy she had never seen before.

His expression changed rapidly into an alarming smirky grin that caught her off guard.

"Well, well, honeymoon over already?"

She felt herself go cold with shock then hot with outrage at this bowlegged punk who she couldn't seem to place.

"I beg your pardon," she grated slowly, her anger firing darts. "Who are you?"

Toni caught the split second flash of nervousness that crossed his face before the smirk returned.

"Names Joe. I heard Luke got himself hitched. Congratulations." He took a few steps closer to her hay bale seductively holding her gaze. "Or maybe not. You look like you're needing a friend." He was sneering and his offer of friendship made Toni's skin prickle.

"No!" she retorted, "actually *alone* is what I need. What are you doing here?"

Alarm flickered only a moment, but she saw it. "Uh, Mr. Luke asked me to check on the, uh, a little filly's leg. She sprained it yesterday."

"Oh?" Toni forgot her tortured heart for the moment, but her thoughts didn't turn toward the filly. She stood up abruptly.

This guy wasn't adding up. "I don't remember seeing you working here."

His expression darkened. "Part time. I work part time, when the boss needs me. I'll just have a quick look-see."

Discounting his credibility now, she suddenly turned in front of him and headed toward the stalls on the far side of the barn.

0   "No!" he blurted nervously. "You'll just scare her if you rush up on her. I'll go."

She stopped and turned to look him in the eye. "I'll see for myself, thank you." Judd hadn't mentioned the filly but she hadn't exactly been involved with the ranch happenings up until now. But Joe *whoever* didn't know that. She wheeled around toward the stall, but only managed a step before the toe of her shoe caught on a bent piece of baling wire and sent her reeling forward. It was the thought of re-injuring the arm that caused her to shriek. His quick agility brought her upright again and he kept his long bony arm secured tightly around her waist for a few seconds it took her to regain a sense of balance.

But those few impersonal seconds were obviously misinterpreted by the larger than life figure that had just appeared in the doorway. Toni went pale at the cold glare of anger painted like a rubber mask on Judd's face.

Reading her face, the cowboy flinched and wheeled around as though a blow had already been thrown at him.

Hours seemed to pass before a word was spoken, giving Toni time to remember where Judd had been all evening and felt her anger rising to meet the fury of her husbands, a fury that Toni could only contribute to a deflated ego in the face of one of his Double OO hands.

A sort of revengeful pleasure rose inside her at Judd's obvious misinterpretation of her being in another man's arms, but the stockman's job, if not his life was on the line and she would have to clear it up quickly.

"Judd, it's not..."

"Shut up," he stormed, staring now at the cowboy with murder in his eyes. "Go to the house, Toni." He was still glowering at the ashen faced Joe.

"I'm not going anywhere until you understand what..."

Before she could finish, Judd reached her in a couple of strides and grasped her good arm helping her none too gently toward the door.

"Go!"

Toni waited to hear no more, but ran out through the darkness as soon as he let go of her. She had taken the brunt of Judd's anger before but this time it was different. She was truly scared of the savagery that gripped him and once she closed the door of the guest room behind herself, it was some minutes before she could stop her body from shaking. She had no idea why she chose the guest room other than it seemed to set her apart somewhat.

She lowered the window blind to shut out the moonlight and lay across the bed feeling as dark and lonely as the blackness in the room. Her mind swept over the memories over the weeks after they had first made love. Almost like two teenagers making up for the loss of *silly* time, they laughed and played and ran through the house playing chase. They had offered their bodies to each other with uninhibited abandon, taking and giving until both were satiated with physical and emotional contentment.

But now, lying dazed and numb in the dark, her lungs felt like they had deflated. She couldn't just stop loving this man and the thought of him not being an integral part of her daily existence was as unacceptable to her as allowing his abusive behavior. She believed he loved her. If he was faking those emotions, the man had certainly missed his calling as an actor.

She had read once that life is a marathon, not a sprint. You set yourself in for the long haul in order to complete your full destiny. But, had she taken a wrong turn somewhere? No. Even in the shallow end of her heart, she knew that wasn't it. She was where she belonged. She just wasn't getting the whole picture concerning this Maggie woman.

Anyway, it was she who should be angry, who held the whip hand in this situation. She had done nothing wrong, but she knew right where to put her hands on the evidence to prove Judd had lied to her. So why didn't she just stick the letter under his nose and demand an explanation?

She blinked at the stream of salt water and felt it drip down onto her hair. She knew why she wouldn't. Chancing him admitting his love for another woman would mean an immediate end to her hopes of winning. Possibly her hopes were in vain now, but she wasn't ready to let go.

The back door slammed hard and Toni held her breath as heavy footsteps approached and stopped outside her door. Her heart hammered until her chest hurt in anticipation of a scene with a raging bull. But when the steps retreated and she heard *their* bedroom door slam, she felt, not relief, but, hurt and rejected.

Judd's disposition didn't seem to have altered when he burst into the guest room the next morning. His muted, "Good God!" at the sight of her curled up in a ball on the bed still fully dressed, brought her upright.

She wanted to close her eyes against the frigid gaze digging into her. "What time is it?" she asked sleepily, not really caring. She was trembling slightly, expecting any second to be lashed at with questions about last night.

Instead, he spoke very casually, contradicting the flashing anger in his eyes. "Nine-thirty. You better get a move on. Your cast comes off at eleven."

"But that's not until tomorrow."

"I had it changed."

"Any particular reason why?"

"You'll see." He left abruptly.

With her heart wrapped around her ankles, Toni knew there was nothing to do at this point but comply.

The trip to town and back was silently strained and Toni resented Judd's formal attitude. It was as though nothing intimately good had ever passed between them.

But for every painful and degrading moment of the past hours, it didn't prepare her for Judd's, *you'll see,* which was announced abruptly as they entered the front door.

Her first reaction was surprise. Then distrust after Judd's disclosure that he had fired Joe a month ago who wasn't Joe at all but a drifter named Martin Call. And now he suggested, rather demanded, that since she had been released from the doctor's care, that she take over the responsibilities that Mr. Call left behind.

"That's what you really want, isn't it?" He watched her narrowly.

"Well, yes. I mean...I..."

"I know what you mean," he shot sarcastically. "Get your boots on." He stalked off toward the kitchen leaving her to stare after him open mouthed.

All kinds of notions were whirling in Toni's mind. Judd was still angry with her, unwarranted as it was, and this little act of giving her what she really wanted was derived out of his need to punish her. Well, the truth always comes out eventually, she knew. And while she waited for her ship to come in, she planned to immensely enjoy the wait, despite the heaviness in her heart.

Judd was nowhere in sight when Toni emerged from the bedroom ready for whatever was waiting for her out the back door. Her white short sleeved v-neck T might not be the best work shirt, but Toni was about comfort today. She had tucked the bottom of her Faded Glory Jeans into the top of black roper boots.

The sun was high and warm and she bounded out into the middle of it. She caught a glimpse of Judd carrying a bucket across the arena, then disappear into the barn.

She entered the side door and immediately felt her self-assurance slipping at the penetrating blue ice flickering over her ranch hand attire.

"If it's me you're trying to impress, don't waste your time again."

She sighed heavily, not wanting to argue. "Please, Cowboy."

"Please, Cowboy, what!" he taunted. "It's obvious where your interest lies, but you'll soon find you've hired on with the wrong outfit. Here." He tossed the plastic pail at her.

She responded automatically and jerked her freshly mended arm up to catch it. A fierce pain stabbed around her elbow making her wince.

Regret flashed almost urgently to Judd's face as he took a stride toward her, but Toni grasped the pail firmly and stepped back.

Just tell me what you want done with this," she grouched at him.

His eyes narrowed on her, giving her a quick once over. "The feed is in that bin. Give the rest of those colts a scoop each. I'll help you with the hay."

"I don't need your help. Just give me my job description and you can go on about your own business."

He regarded her silently, his expression changing to cool amusement. "As you wish," slipped out of the side of his mouth.

Toni felt her nerves tighten knowing he expected to find a half-baked job done at the end of the day. Judd immediately rattled off an itinerary for her that would take a hyperactive muscle man a week to complete. She lifted her hand in mock salute when he had finished and marched very capably to the feed bin. She measured four scoops into the bucket and turned to find herself alone.

"Jerk," she muttered, knowing he was trying to make a fool of her. I'll make a show place of this barn if it kills me, she promised herself, knowing it full well might. The place was a disaster.

Angry determination pushed Toni through several hours of raking and sweeping and restacking hay. The root of her anger being the nagging thoughts of the faceless woman named Maggie. The shock and humiliation rushed over her again and again and she worked feverishly in an effort to drive away the torment. Exactly what she hoped to accomplish by working herself to the bone, she didn't know, except that this job would give her reason to stay and keep her out of open competition with Maggie...for the time being. Time was her best ally now and she planned to use it.

Finally when she felt her body couldn't produce another second of labor, Toni plopped down on a hay bale and gave herself a needed pat on the back. She pulled a wadded paper towel from her back pocket and wiped the muddy sweat from her face. She leaned back exhausted, and listened to the soft nickering of the colts in their stalls. Then it dawned on her that she hadn't cleaned the two empty stalls on the far side of the barn. They'll have to wait, she decided, before a mental image of a triumphant *I told you so* smirk on Judd Luke's face brought her to her feet. Not on her barely sustained life would she give him that pleasure.

It was almost an hour later when she wheel-barrowed the last load of wood shavings in and spread it evenly in the vacant stalls. She had noticed earlier that the four stalls corralling the colts were in terrible need of cleaning but the animals would have to be moved out first. Judd hadn't mentioned these stalls and that seemed to be all the reason she needed to muster the strength to do them.

Toni took a deep breath, then haltered each of the fidgeting babies, leading them one by one to a hot walker behind the barn. She noticed the little filly didn't seem to be favoring a limb, but was the most feisty and fit of the group. The thrill of handling the horses again seemed to rush a new enthusiasm into her tired body. She worked diligently until all four stalls were clean and new bedding was hauled in and spread.

After the last colt had been returned to its quarters, Toni sighed in weary relief and put away her equipment. She emerged from the barn to find the sun setting behind the trees in the far distance. She doubted that she had ever known real exhaustion before now. Each step she took toward the house felt like a mile. Every bone in her body, including her grimy hair ached.

The house was dark and empty. It took all her strength getting out of her sticky clothes just inside the utility room. Every little crease and tuck in her jeans was filled with hay and sawdust which filled the air and floor as she pulled free of her boots. She peeled her jeans and blouse off, grimacing at the total ruination of her favorite white T shirt. Leaving them in a heap on the floor, she headed for a hot, sudsy bath. The faintest scent of Judd's after shave touched the air in the bathroom and not even an extra douse of fragrant soap could erase the masculine scent from her nostrils.

She soaked for a half hour, agonizing for a half hour whether Judd would even come home tonight. Was he even on the ranch at all? She closed her eyes, resting her head on the back rim of the tub and gave herself over to the memory of their lovemaking...the sweet, soul jarring passion that Judd had evoked and brought to completion for her night after night. She lay beneath the cooling water, quivering, wanting, her mind obsessed by his image. Sighing, she finished her bath with a serious head scrubbing and toweled herself dry. She let her damp hair fall where it chose, tucked a dry towel around herself and headed for the bedroom. Just as she was about to exchange the towel for a more suitable nightgown, Toni jumped at the loud slam of the back door. Footsteps thudded on the tiled floor and Toni reminded herself to accept Judd's appreciation of her day's labor with a graceful thank you...without the smirk.

But the slight smile she intended as a greeting faded on sight of the tall figure of her husband now standing within the door frame. For a moment, Toni clenched her hands at the sharp arrogance in his expression. She forced herself to look straight at him, even though his scowling gaze had left her face and traveled slowly down her slender neck and bare shoulders where damp tendrils of hair clung to her skin. She felt madness well up inside her, a desire to rush into his arms, but she stood still.

At least his appearance answered her question that had tortured her all evening. His clothes were crumpled and dirty, his face coated with a hard days dirt. He certainly hadn't been away with this Maggie all day.

Judd's eyes rested grimly on Toni's face. "Who gave you permission to take those colts out of their stalls?" His voice was dangerously low, his lips barely moving as he spoke.

Toni was stunned. Her eyes widened, sparkling with anger. "Is that *all* you can say about the work I did out there?"

"I didn't tell you to handle those colts." he persisted.

"Their stalls, Judd, were in bad need of cleaning. I had to remove them first. The exercise certainly didn't hurt them."

"Exercise!" he exploded.

She closed her eyes a moment to rein in some control, then looked him square in the eye. "The hot walker, Cowboy. It's a simple procedure."

-336   "Don't patronize me." He thrust a warning finger toward her.

Toni jumped. "I'm sorry. Let's not argue about this. I'm bone tired and I'm going to bed." She snatched a gown from the open chest of drawers and moved toward the doorway. Judd stood still, blocking her exit.

"If you're going to bed, you're headed in the wrong direction."

In her heart, Toni agreed with him. Through the dirt and sweat and anger covering the tall cowboy, Toni saw the tender strength of the only man she had ever wanted. Her pulse missed a beat and it was sheer hell listening to her mind involuntarily recite the letter that was signed...*Maggie*.

"Am I, Cowboy?"

His eyes narrowed as though trying to understand what she meant. Then he stepped aside.

Unhappily Toni trudged to the guest room and sleep finally came after a deluge of tears.

***

CHAPTER EIGHT

Toni awoke early the next morning to a gray overcast sky and body full of aching muscles. Her spirit blended perfectly and a thought crossed her mind which she immediately shook off. Not on a bet would she lay in bed today and endure Judd's *I told you so.*

The house was quiet. She stretched her arm and squinted at the Timex around her wrist. Six o'clock. She lay still a few minutes surprised that Judd hadn't awakened her. The work day usually began an hour ago.

A moan escaped her lips as she swung herself upright and slipped into jeans, boots and a sleeveless cotton shirt. A cold splash of water on her face brought her out of her stupor enough to get a cup of coffee made for herself. She was about to carry it back to her room when she saw with a sudden pounding of her pulse that Judd was blocking the doorway.

He didn't say a word. He just leaned against the door frame and watched her. He was dressed in faded jeans and a worn red plaid shirt. He was clean shaven but his hair was a little rumpled underneath his well-worn straw.

"I thought you were already gone." Toni tried to sound nonchalant. "Have a seat. I'll make another cup of coffee."

"No thanks, I've had mine." He tilted the brim of his hat slightly as if to gain a better view of her. His survey went from head to foot, then solemnly, "Not even a hint of the greenhorn limp. Maybe I should reconsider your worth to the Double OO."

"A good businessman would have done that *before* hiring me," she quipped saucily.

"I didn't seem to have much choice."

"Soft spot for orphans, huh?"

"Among other things."

"Careful. You're getting personal with the help."

Judd's casual bantering with her belied the intensity on his face and when his patience snapped, Toni was prepared and unaffected.

"Damnation, Toni, where is this getting us."

"Late for work is all I can think of. Pitiful example you're setting for the new stockman, uh, stockwoman."

He stared at her unblinking for a few seconds. "Then maybe I'd better do something about that," he ground at her. He flipped off the light switch and motioned toward the back door. "Let's go."

"I'm not quite ready yet." Her hand moved to her sleep tousled hair.

"We're not going on a picnic. If you want to work like a Double OO hand, you'll have to dispense with being a woman."

Calmly she set her coffee cup in the sink and started past him toward the back door, then stopped and looked back at him. "Just for the record, I agree with you one hundred percent. You *are* an ass. A big fat one."

Just before she turned to make a quick exit, she caught sight of the grin pulling on his lips.

Only a necessary exchange of words were made between the two while Judd saddled his gelding, then a young mare.

He handed Toni the gelding's reins. "Mount up and keep a safe distance from this little lady. She likes to play."

The excitement of being caught up in her element after so long was exhilarating for Toni. Only *Maggie* niggling at the back of her mind hampered her complete happiness as she rode with confidence across the looming grassland.

The expression on Judd's masterful tanned face told her he was totally in his element as well, tied by his heart strings to life at the Double OO.

What would it be like, she wondered, to have such a man, her husband, love her with such intensity, with the same fierceness that he loved this land and the lifestyle it demanded. And Maggie. What could this woman give him, even in her absence that Toni Barton Luke couldn't?

Peggy Patrick

Her thoughts had suddenly become distasteful and she pushed them aside savoring the fact that it was she who was with Judd now, sharing the very essence of life that made him the man he was.

As they weaved their way now slowly through the thickening pine forest, Toni strained against the memories of the one time Judd had brought her into this place.

Her attention was thankfully caught by the sound of bawling calves in the distance and finally the shouts and hooting of the cowboys. The mass of pines opened into a clearing of matted wild flowers, reds, yellows, and blues that clung to the slope of a valley that enveloped animals and riders. Judd halted the filly and watched the activity for a few minutes. The noisy bellowing of mothers for their calves and the resounding replies of their offspring echoed across the valley. It was branding time and a childlike excitement rose up in Toni. A covered chuck wagon set at the edge of all the activity surrounded by tents, bedrolls and portable holding pens.

She was so absorbed in the old west scene before her that she started at the way she discovered Judd looking at her. The wondering, boyish expression on his face sent a shiver through her middle.

Judd gently shifted in the saddle and clicked at his mount to move on down the slope. Toni followed, anesthetizing her pain with an anticipation of the work day stretched before her.

"How's it going, Doyle?" Judd called out over the noise to an older dust covered cowboy holding a calf to the ground.

"Morning, Boss. Rain holds off a few hours and we'll be in fine shape."

Toni stopped beside Judd just in time to see the hot iron make its mark at the hands of A.J., his jaw puffed out with chewing tobacco. The burning calf hide and bawl of the young animal made her cringe.

"Morning, ma'am." Doyle nodded and smiled admiringly at Toni.

"Toni, Doyle Williamson is one of the best cattlemen in this country." Judd bragged with great pride, allowing his softer side to peek out.

The old man's modesty pinked through the brown soot that smeared his weathered cheeks as he swallowed Toni's hand inside his big cowhide glove. "Nice to see you again, Mrs. Luke.

"It's Toni, Doyle. Thanks." She nodded and smiled, wondering at the sweetness of these older cowboys. For all their tough, male exteriors, Doyle, like Sky Cooper, exhibited a humble gentle heart that would melt any woman in her boots. But neither was married, except to the cowboy life. Maybe they were happier this way, but her sappy romantic heart couldn't quite believe that.

"Toni's of a mind to learn something of the ranching business," Judd said.   There's no better way to learn than to jump in with both feet. Isn't that right, honey?"

She bit her lower lip and swallowed hard. He was making fun of her now, having her centered in his testosterone charged territory.

She flashed Judd a warning smile. "That's right, sweetheart. Both feet."

He reined away and gestured her to follow. She was conscious of the heads turning as she waited for a safe distance to move in behind Judd's mount.

Toni's first impulse of excitement changed over the next few hours to dismay. Judd had left her on patrol instructing her to walk the gelding slowly back and forth to settle the herd. Out of shape was putting her riding condition mildly.

The morning passed and the clanging bell to *come and get it* from the old chuck wagon was a welcomed relief for Toni from tons of blowing dust, bawling calves and an aching backside.

A young cowboy motioned her toward the wagon and took over her position.

Toni hadn't imagined what strength of body was necessary to carry out the simplest task in this world of man and beast. She was just realizing how pampered she had been by Uncle John during her work days on his ranch. When she got tired, he would send her to the house. She was weaker physically than she dared admit and with head held high, she dismounted beside the wagon where Judd already held a hot plate of food ready for her.

"How's it going?" he chirped, eyeing her with some strange satisfied glint.

"Oh, I've hardly stuck my second foot in yet," she cooed. Actually she was butt deep and sinking.

He continued to watch her as she thanked him for the plate and sat down cross legged on the hard ground a private distance from the growing crowd. He joined her after a moment.

"If I didn't know better, I'd almost believe you really were enjoying these grueling hours in the saddle."

"And just exactly *what* do you know?"

"That there are only two good reasons a woman would want to work like a man. Either she possesses more masculine traits than feminine ones, or she just enjoys attracting attention from men. It's not hard to figure which way it is."

"That's unfair," she shot back defensively. "Did it ever once occur to you that I might just enjoy riding? That does not make me masculine nor a flirt. Anyway, there is certainly nothing wrong with a woman giving her husband a helping hand."

"You didn't have a husband when you came here. And it's obvious you're not particularly choosy about the company you keep."

A scathing contempt filled his eyes and Toni went cold all over. Martin Call.

"You didn't give me a chance to explain."

"There was no need. Martin was a thief. That line he fed you about the injured filly was a cover up."

Toni's mouth dropped open. "You were there all that time. Then you know there was nothing going on between..."

"All I know is, I didn't give it the chance. You called to him and his arms came around you. Only you will ever know what might have happened next. What you *wanted* to happen next."

"Oh!" she cried, more hurt than angry. "You sound like the almighty voice of experience, but then maybe you've earned it."

"What are you talking about?"

"She knew she was standing one step off of the finish line, but control had slipped away. "Your so-called business meeting," she stated flatly.

-336   "I told you all you need to know about that. It was strictly a personal business matter that concerns me."

"And Maggie?" She could have ripped her tongue out then, but instead prayed for strength as she watched Judd's face tighten.   He set his tin plate down, took hers, and chunked it on top of his.

He stood and forcefully pulled her to her feet, no patience in him for her muffled protest. "Where did you hear about Maggie? His eyes were flashing.

"What difference does it...ah?"

He squeezed her arm. "Don't push me. Tell me who told you."

"You're hurting me, Judd." Her eyes welled and she felt his grip loosen. She swallowed, deeply regretting her revelation about Maggie, but she had no choice now but to finish it.

"I...I was looking for something to read while you were gone. Her letter was on the fax and...I read it. You were with Maggie that night weren't you?"

Her heart begged for a denial, but his expression told her she wouldn't get it.

His hands dropped away from her. His eyes clouded and drifted far away. "Yes, I was."

She thought he would walk away from her then and it would be finished. But he didn't. Surprisingly, he reached for her hand and held it very tightly. Her heart seemed to stop at the sudden intensity of his look, then began pounding in a mixture of anger and unhappiness.

For a few seconds, the world became silent to the sounds of cattle and cowboys. There was only the two of them. She could almost hear the desperate cry of his heart.

Thunder boomed around them suddenly. Curses, shouts and pounding hoofs ended the moment and sent them both back to work to help gather the frightened cattle scattering across the valley.

The afternoon was long and tiring. The big gelding was restless, seeming to sense Toni's emotional struggle. Judd had not ridden near her and she thought she should head for home and straight out of Judd Luke's life. Pride should have given her the push she needed, but where Cowboy was concerned, she couldn't muster it up. Once again, Uncle John was pulling at her memory. *Grab hold and never let go.*

For a few moments, bitterness waved through her mind...bitter that she had allowed those words to smother her self-respect. But her Baxter blood was stubbornly thick.

She watched the lean figure of Judd in the distance bending almost casually with the quick movements of the animal carrying him. It was like looking back in time. She had watched him ride hundreds of times, admired the natural motion of his body on horseback, and loved him as a 14 year old girl loves. The past stirred to life within her and she wanted to cry for that innocent young love that grew into a woman seemingly bent on self-destruction.

She didn't know how she got through the last couple of hours astride the saddle, but the thought of a hot sudsy bath and soft cool sheets helped her sit contently beside the chuck wagon waiting for Judd to talk over the day's work with his hands.

Soon he brought her the news that he would have to stay on watch tonight until the threat of the storm passed.

"Can't take a chance on getting this herd scattered," his tone was all business.

Toni stood, biting her lip against a moan of muscle cramps. "That's ok. I can find my way home."

"You're staying here with me. Our tent is up on that ridge." His hand waved toward the hill behind the chuck wagon. "Come on. I'll show you."

She blinked and stared at his back as he walked away expecting her to follow without question. She was caked with dirt, sweat and cow poop and bone tired and he expected her to take this?

When she didn't move, he stopped and turned his head around. Tired, pallid, blue ice regarded her. "Are you coming?" A smirk pulled his lips. "Or do you need help?"

That did it. With her little remaining strength and will to live, she trudged up the embankment behind him.

The tent was larger than she expected and looked like it had been there a while. Faded work jeans and shirts were waded among an assortment of things in a cardboard box that set beneath a short canopy.

Everything you'll need is here. Make yourself at home." He left.

No sympathy whatsoever, she grumbled to herself. Maybe if I'd been born a cow...She wondered what he expected her to make her supper out of before she fished a jar of peanut butter and baggie of crackers out of the box. What more could a body want?

Gazing around the one-tent campground, she found she was quite isolated and within an hour of total darkness.

Inside the tent, she sluiced her face in a bucket of water then spent ten minutes getting the Coleman lantern hanging above her head lit. Then it dawned on her that the creek was not too far away. With the lantern in hand, she found a beaten path leading into the trees behind the tent. The trail seemed to go on and on, feeling more desolate with each step until she could hear a faint rippling sound. She quickened her pace and the next moment saw the pool. The darkness hid the circle of pines on the opposite bank, but she saw them clearly. The honeymoon hideaway.

Now her desolation was complete.

She refused to think, but set the lantern at the edge of the pool and stripped off her clothes. She eased in slowly closing out everything from her mind...her hunger, her aching heart and welcomed the numbing sensation of the cold water.

She turned over and floated on her back, oblivious to her exposed nakedness. She swam lazily to the trickling waterfall and lifted herself upon the flat surfaced rock in the midst of it, the gentle force of water massaging the stiffness from her thighs and legs.

She hadn't considered that she was so nakedly exposed until she saw the glow of a small flashlight in the shadows of the trees. Her heart jerked in fear and she quickly eased herself into the water. Did the hands use this place? Where were her clothes? Where was her *brain*? Her clothes were out of reach and no one could possibly hear her this far away. She sunk up to her chin and remained still.

The light disappeared and a faint rustling sound echoed in her ears. Then to her utter horror, a pair of boots and pieces of clothing were tossed from the shadows on top of her own clothing. Toni held her breath thinking if worse came to worse she could drown herself.

Then she let out her breath slowly, raggedly as she watched the lithe naked form of her husband walk from the shadows and enter the pool without a word. His eyes never left hers even as he glided across the deepest center of the pool and finally stood in the waist deep water in front of her. His face drawn with some inner sadness, he circled large hands around her waist and lifted her to her feet. Gently, slowly he drew her closer to him until she was overwhelmingly conscious of his hard muscles and warm naked skin. His arms came around her back and pressed her fully against him, gradually tightening his hold until she thought the very life would be crushed from her.

Toni heard him sigh softly as a whirl of emotions threatened to smother her. Neither spoke, but he held her and held her as she thought of all the things that had passed between them since her arrival at the ranch, especially her vow to make him love her. Only her.

Yet she knew that her love for this man was meshed into her body, her mind, her spirit until not even death could betray it. Had Judd already stepped across that same irrevocable line with a woman he couldn't possess?

Toni felt his hold slacken and he was kissing her lips with the same urgency that his arms had possessed.

Calloused hands lowered to grip her thighs beneath the dark night water. He pressed her tightly against himself.

In spite of her own aroused flesh, her emotions remained in chaos. Whether she allowed him to make love to her now or not would not erase the knowledge wedged between their hearts. She couldn't dismiss the whole thing as Judd apparently was attempting to do and she found she was suddenly pushing against his unyielding strength.

"Stop it, Judd." she cried.

He released her and looked at her hard, his expression...could it be pain? No, not pain. His macho image was just a little bent out of shape.

"Maybe you were expecting someone else?" he snarled at her.

"Oh," she seethed, glaring angrily up at him. "How dare *you* make such a remark to *me.*!"

Suddenly she was ashamed of standing nude in front of those glittering and now contemptuous eyes. She scrambled out of the water and retrieved her clothing.

Toni's hands shook until she was barely able to button her blouse. Eyes blinded with tears, she hadn't realized Judd was dressed again and watching her. Humiliated and sickened, she felt a wild surge of anger sweep her remaining bits of patience to the wind.

"I'm leaving, Judd. Buy yourself a nice quiet little divorce and do it right away please. I have a life to get on with and you can pick up wherever you left off with Maggie what's-her-name!"

She started past him but was stopped and held solidly in place. His hands rested on her shoulders with a gentle pressure.

 A muscle worked in the side of his jaw, but Toni saw fear in his widened eyes. "You are not going anywhere and there won't be a divorce. I gave you your chance to leave and you refused it. Remember?"

She forced a shaky "yes" around the swell in her throat. "I...I would like to go back to the house."

He released her and picked up the lantern and took the lead toward the trail stopping a moment to cut Toni a quick sideways glance and proclaim, "Her name is Maggie Luke."

***

CHAPTER NINE

Maggie Luke was undoubtedly beautiful, an ash blonde woman with china doll features. But the posed smile fixed on her small mouth seemed to accentuate an unmistakable hardness in her eyes. There was no indication how long ago the picture was taken, but the signature across the bottom left no mistake about her identity.

It had taken a full twenty-four hours to unthaw the shock of Judd's one-line revelation that she was his ex-wife. Toni's emotions were worse than shredded, but her Baxter blood was pumping to the tune of a blowout and only an act of God could prevent her from acting on her secret declaration of war.

Darkness had fallen and she hadn't seen her husband since he'd driven her home last evening. The threat of rain had passed over hours ago, but she doubted the weather had anything to do with his absence.

She slid the photograph back inside the bottom desk drawer feeling no guilt at meddling in Judd's private quarters.

She jumped when the phone rang only inches from her ear and grabbed it to prevent another deafening ring.

A moment later, Toni hung up feeling as if she'd been doused with ice water. A motel phone service had left a message for J. Vincent Luke that Maggie would arrive at the ranch tomorrow morning as scheduled.

God, was she a total fool? Was she waging war against a woman who had won a long time ago?

Unhappily, she dragged herself to bed in the guest room, defeated and washed out. But sleep eluded her as a mental war raged inside her head...planning, calculating, one ridiculous scheme after another...none that seemed befitting to a civilized human being.

When she had inwardly exhausted her anger toward the ex-Mrs. Luke, a more rational idea occurred. Maybe if she simply swallowed her pride and showed Judd exactly how much she loved him. Wasn't true love supposed to conquer all? *Love never fails. That's a promise. God's promise.*

A light switched on in her mind. With an exuberant rush of strength, Toni got up, showered and dressed, intentionally leaving off any binding underclothes. She used the blower on her hair and applied makeup. A light spray of Heaven Scent trailed her outside where she climbed into the ranch pick-up and retraced the route Judd had taken in the jeep to bring her home the night before.

It was a much shorter distance to the valley by road. She felt herself trembling as she neared the campsite. It had only been a few hours since she'd told Cowboy she was leaving him. How would he react to her complete turnaround?

Her mind went briefly to Uncle John. What would he have thought to see his favorite tomboy lay all her pride aside and run dementedly after a man, hungering for his hands on her body, his lips pressed to hers? *Never let go,* he had said. Something stirred deep within Toni as she recalled those words. Somehow she knew John Baxter was at that moment smiling.

Toni pulled up beside Judd's jeep a few feet from the trail leading up to his tent. Noticing the lantern light was on inside, she took a deep breath and started up. Her legs felt strangely awkward, as though they didn't belong to her. But she continued. Her heart bumped up in her throat as she reached flat ground. She found Judd standing in the tent door frowning.

"Toni! What are you doing out here this time of night?" He gave her no time to answer but quickly stepped aside. "Come inside." He followed her in and closed the heavy canvas flap at the entrance before turning toward her.

Something in his gaze that roamed her hair and face caused the color to rise in Toni's cheeks. He looked rough and overpoweringly male. He was unshaven and still wearing his hat. His shirt was unsnapped to where it tucked into dusty jeans.

He shifted his lean weight, making the jangle of his spurs sound like a whip-crack in the stillness.

They stared openly at each other for a long moment. His gaze fell and steeled on her chest and she knew her bra-less form was protruding against her T-shirt.

Flames of open passion leaped in his eyes and Toni gave silent consent. Pride had no place left in her where her husband was concerned.

"Judd," she began, but strong arms were suddenly around her, molding her slight body to a hard, protective warmness.

"Shhh. I don't want words. I want you. Just you."

Her whole being…mind, body and spirit answered, *yes,* as she received his kiss and gave back with every thread of her heart exposed.

He released his hold on her long enough to toss his hat away and turn down the lantern. Gently he guided her down to a thickness of blankets and stretched out beside her, his rough calloused hands searching the smooth skin beneath her shirt as his mouth moved hungrily on hers.

A sweet delirious yearning washed through her as she responded, pulling him closer. He pulled her skimpy, low-cut T over her head, teasing her with kisses on her cheek and down her throat.

"Cowboy," she moaned, saturated with an aching need that was making her crazy.

He unfastened her jeans and slid them down and off, then stood and removed his own clothes. She reached for him as he came back to her. She felt him tremble as she ran her fingers across his bare shoulders and through the fine swirls of hair on his chest.

SURRENDERED

Reaching to hold his face between her hands, she drew him to her and kissed him. An arm slid beneath her and as he rolled to lay flat on his back, she was lifted on top of him.

Her own passion blazed as she felt his heart pounding erratically. He wanted her to take the lead, to love him. And she held nothing back…touching him, feeling every earth shaking tremble in his body echo back to her, urging murmurs of love words that poured from the depths of her being.

Suddenly he rolled her onto her back. Toni couldn't have imagined there could be more to Judd's lovemaking than she had experienced in times past. But tonight he seemed to be trying to convey a deeper message to her. In the filtered moonlight, Toni's eyes locked with Judd's as he lifted himself and joined their bodies, his eyes conveying the depth of his soul even as a slow, sensuous rhythm rocked them into oblivion.

He shuddered against her already spent, drowsy form, relaxing a moment before rolling off of her. His arm rested heavily against her stomach, but tightened when she attempted to move.

"Don't leave me, baby." he whispered, pleading.

She rolled to her side and gave him the tight security of her arms.

"What would I do without my little cowgirl? Don't ever go away." He kissed the tip of her nose and stroked her hair.

There was nothing to compare to the sweetness of the moment for Toni. The scheduled arrival of Maggie was forgotten as was every dark cloud that ever descended upon her.

Judd's breathing rhythm told her he was asleep.

"I'll never let go, Cowboy." she murmured softly.

"Toni..." she heard Judd's voice, but from a distance.

Turning her face upward, she squinted at him standing just inside the tent flap, fully dressed. She could tell the morning sun was already bright.

"Judd, why didn't you wake me sooner." Waking in their love nest all alone was disappointing, but the more than annoyed crease in Judd's brow disturbed her more. "What is it?" She sat up. A quilt Judd had obviously thrown over her during the night slipped to her lap, exposing her.

A quivering sigh heaved Judd's chest. His mixed expression of indecision and confusion bewildered Toni.

"Judd?"

"Get dressed and wait here for me. Something's come up at the house. I'll be right back." He wheeled and was gone.

She stared in confusion at the flap of canvas still vibrating behind him until she remembered. Maggie. He certainly didn't let his shirt-tail touch him, she fumed.

Toni sat on the blankets, face in her hands. Should she jump up and run after him like her insides were rioting at her to do? Or sit there like a mannequin and wait for the happy couple to kiss and reunite.

Three minutes later, Toni exited the tent. The flatbed was still parked in the back of the tent, but Judd's horse was gone.

She had to find out the truth. She had every right to be included in this little *get-together*. *She* was Judd's wife.

Before she could get backed out of the narrow path in the trees, her name carried in the wind from somewhere.

"Toni! "

It was Doyle Williamson. Toni put the truck in park and waited for him to reach her.

"Hey there, young lady. Wondered if you could do an old man a favor?" His eyes twinkled beneath his hat brim.

"Sure I can, Doyle." She tried to cheerfully cover the turmoil boiling beneath her surface.

"Judd said he'd be home most of the morning. Wondered if you'd mind seein' he gets this." He handed her a folded scrap of paper through the window. "Measurements he asked me to get for him."

"I'd be happy to."

"I'm guessing you know the easiest way around to the house by now? Going through the pastures and gates is more trouble than taking the longer way around the road."

Confused, Toni shook her head slowly trying to follow what he was saying. The ranch house was almost a straight shot from here. No gates.

He saw her confusion. "Cross the cattle guard there in front of J.V.'s home place and go right, bout two miles turn on the first road again right and watch for a new road that winds through the trees there. Just follow it until you see the gate. Remember it now?

"Yes. Yes, thank you, Doyle."

"Preciate it. Good day now." He ambled back down the hill toward the herd.

Toni closed her eyes and felt numb all over. All the air around her seemed to have been breathed up. Doyle had just told her how to drive around to Judd's house? That beautiful log dream home was Judd's. Her husband's. That answered questions about where he disappeared at times, where he managed to clean up and come *home* dressed in clean pressed clothes. But it didn't tell her why he never told her or took her there.

She jerked upright at the next thought. Was that his and Maggie's home? She realized then that she was driving, nearly home. But she didn't stop there. She followed the map drawn in her head from Doyle's directions and presently found herself at the gate entrance to the LUKE house.

Toni's mouth dried up and her heart began to pound as she pulled up beside a late model silver Lincoln Continental. Her wrinkled glue-eyed appearance was suddenly magnified by the whole picture of wealth and glitz surrounding her.

What would she accomplish by barging in on...on what? Her hands squeezed the steering wheel until her knuckles turned white. After the hot rush of anger subsided, she rested her head on the wheel and deliberately remembered every detail of the past night, the wanting, the loving, the sweetness of Judd's body joined with hers. And the purest of love and devotion he had poured out of his spirit into hers as their bodies came together. It was difficult to believe he could love another woman, and express such fervent passion for her at the same time. Could it be possible for a man to be in love with two women at once? No! The thought tore at Toni's soul. Salty droplets of water dripped, her insides were running away screaming.

The momentum carried her, almost without effort, up the grey slate steps to the massive natural wood double doors. She didn't knock. The doors opened easily and quietly. She left them part way open as she took in the rich interior details. The décor was so like the man who owned it - rich polished log rafters blended with old barn wood walls and trim of hand-hewn timber. Comfortably luxurious, the home exuded a real western ambiance.

Muted voices sifted through a half opened interior door, moving her forward, but she stopped outside the door when the voices became clearer.

"Oh, Vinny. I can't believe all that has happened." A woman's soft voice choked emotionally. "Your love is all that matters to me. That Will caused so much trouble. The marriage demand. I'm to blame for that. If you hadn't come home to me...forgiven me..."

Judd's voice intermingled with the feminine one in low, gravelly murmurings. Woodenly, Toni moved toward the doorway, feeling that she would see the woman in Judd's arms. The thought of it hurt, but when she actually saw her Cowboy's arms willingly wrapped around a petite blonde woman who was nestled into his chest, she felt stricken.   Toni tried to assimilate all that she'd overheard the woman say. Those words, coupled with the sight before her, was too much.

She stepped quietly backward, then fled from the house to the truck and sat rigidly behind the wheel. Her mind was the only moving part of her and all that it would register was Maggie's words to Judd. *The Will. The marriage demand.* Toni's heart felt cold and that seemed to be the only feeling she had.

Toni sat staring out of the windshield without seeing the brilliant wild flowers patched in front of her. The sky was clear and blue, but she hadn't noticed that either.

She drove home. Didn't hurry. Didn't think. There was no feeling. Just reflex action as she gathered the things she had come with. There was a pleasantness about moving around like a robot, without a mind, without thoughts that tear at the heart.

With three suitcases and cash from the box in the desk, Toni drove the truck to the road, wondering only casually where she was going. The airport would be nice. She could leave the flatbed there and have the airport notify the ranch of its whereabouts. The ranch. She couldn't even *think* his name.

Being back in Dallas felt strange. The crowd at the airport was too noisy. The city lights were too bright and the cab driver was weaving in and out of traffic like a madman.

It was late in the evening when she rang Julie's doorbell, almost hoping she wasn't home. She didn't want to talk. But when the door swung open and that excited familiar face welcomed her, Toni began to *feel* for the first time since early that morning.

"Toni!" Julie exclaimed. "What on earth are you doing here?" Her joy quieted somewhat when she noticed the suitcases stacked on the steps.

Toni could only nod, a lump blocking any words.

"Oh, honey, come in here." Both girls scooped up the bags. Julie gave her a quick hug. "I'll make us some coffee, then we'll talk."

A few minutes later, Toni began to unburden herself, not fully conscious of how desperately she needed the sympathetic ear of another woman.

Julie listened in virtual silence for nearly two hours before Toni finally tilted her head back to rest it on the back of the couch.

"And here I am," she concluded, closing her eyes, relishing the drugged effect that spilling her guts brought. Blessed emptiness.

For a long moment, Julie said nothing, but stared at the wetness soaking Toni's face. It occurred to her then that she'd never seen her cry in all their years as friends. Toni had always been the strong one, brushing off pain and frustration like a pesky fly. Julie had always counted on Toni to bluntly tell her how nobody respected a cry bag; to buck up and go get what she wanted or find a suitable replacement, but for Pete's sake, don't cry about it! Her rock was breaking in front of her and she felt inadequate, even angry.

Julie cocked her head to one side and eyed her friend thoughtfully. "Well, it certainly sounds as if your life has been anything but dull. Have any idea where you lost them?"

Toni jerked her head up, frowning. "Lost what?"

"Your guts. You know the old grit that Toni Barton was famous for. Remember your little motto you used to sing song to me every time I tried to soak your shoulder?"

"No guts, no glory," Toni grinned ruefully, surprised by her friends strong arm tactics.

"Exactly. Now unless you skipped some important details, your story had some holes in it. Forgive me, but it sounded to me like you may have drawn a few conclusions without all the facts."

"You should have been a lawyer." Toni spoke a little sharply.

"I'm sorry," Julie amended. "I don't mean to be so blunt, but maybe you should have asked Judd point blank what this Maggie was to him."

Toni was momentarily back standing in the door of the study, watching Cowboy and Maggie embrace each other's bodies and hearing loudly in her mind, *the will demanded this marriage.*

The cramp in her fingers where she held a death-grip on her coffee mug eased her back to Dallas.

"I think, Julie," she spoke slow and painfully, "that I would have had to be deaf and blind not to have understood."

A lump caught in Toni's throat. She wanted to think that Julie was right, that her eyes had deceived her, that Maggie's words hadn't proved that his heart belonged to the other woman.

Suddenly, she didn't want to talk about Cowboy or Maggie.

Sensing the mood change, Julie gratefully switched and began the saga of the past months in the life of Julie Langston.

It was almost midnight when Toni snapped off the lamp and snuggled under a quilt on the couch. It was painfully clear that she had made a mistake running to Julie with her dangling heart strings. She felt years older than Julie. She had expected her to understand things that only experience could teach. The adolescent problems the pair had confided to each other in years past belonged to another lifetime.

She slept fitfully, fragments of frightening dreams torturing her throughout the night. She felt anything but rested when she awoke to a hazy sunlight peeking through partially opened window shutters.

The apartment was silent, but it was after eight so she assumed Julie had left for work. A hot shower and a sweetened cup of coffee revived her enough to at least make a decision about what to do first. She needed an immediate paycheck. She could be choosey about her line of work later.

Before noon, Toni was the new hostess for the Broiler Steak House located three blocks from the apartment.

"It's almost like old times," Toni quipped too cheerfully to Julie over supper that evening. A bite of bacon and tomato sandwich stuck in her throat at her own revelation that she was back in Dallas as though nothing had changed. *Everything* had changed. It *wasn't* like old times.

She felt numb as she excused herself for bed. Her appetite changed into a tight lump in her throat and Julie was wise enough to keep silent.

Toni awoke with barely enough time to dress and make her ten o'clock shift on time. She had been use to waking at dawn at the ranch. She couldn't seem to get enough sleep now, but she passed that off along with the lightheaded swoon when she sat up that morning as the effects of too much stress on an empty stomach.

Toni worked her shift as well as the next one. The turnover in personnel at the steak house left little to be said for its managers, but Toni seized the opportunity to pull two paychecks since she only had herself to look after.

Thus, her life took on a work and sleep routine that thankfully left her no time to think. Her only communication with Julie was through notes left on the kitchen table.

Finally, after five weeks, the bony-finger schedule had taken its toll. She ignored the recurring dizzy spells that plagued her the past couple of weeks until the morning when she was barely able to reach the bathroom before she threw up.

Weak and miserable, she collapsed back onto her sofa bed and dropped back off to sleep. It was almost noon when the phone awakened her. She remembered telling someone from the restaurant she was sick. Even though the nausea was gone, a drugging sleepiness sent her back to bed.

She was sitting cross-legged in the middle of the couch wondering what time it was when Julie came breezing in from work. The sight sitting on the couch stopped her in her tracks.

"My word, girl. I would swear the cat dragged you in, if I had a cat," she laughed, until a closer look at her friend changed her amusement into concern. "Toni, are you all right?"

"Yes, no..." She felt slightly disoriented. "What are you doing home? What time is it?"

Julie stared at her unbelieving. "It's five-thirty. Have you been asleep all day?"

"Sure looks like it. Wow." Toni massaged her face. "I feel like I've been hit by a truck."

A grin laced with a smirk aimed down at her.

"Looks that way, too, huh?" She managed a half-hearted smile. "Guess I better hit the shower."

"Good girl. I'll fix us something to eat."

"Must have been a twenty-four hour bug or something," Toni said between mouthfuls of mashed potato. She couldn't remember when she had been so hungry.

Julie laughed. "Well, I wouldn't say you're completely back, but you're getting there. Oh," she reached into the deep pocket of her skirt, "I almost forgot. This was in the mailbox."

Julie slid an envelope across the table to her and watched shock leap into her face.

"I couldn't help but notice the return name on it," Julie admitted. "What could Maggie possibly have to say to you?"

Toni shrugged wondering how she knew where to find her. She realized that she hadn't spared a single thought to Maggie in weeks. A surge of bitter anger welled up inside Toni for a woman she had never met. "There's only one way to find out?"

She slit open the envelope with her butter knife and skimmed the short letter. Maggie would be in Dallas on Tuesday and asked Toni to call her at the Marriott, room 212.

The letter stated it was urgent that she speak with Toni as soon as possible.

"That means she arrived yesterday," Julie said after hearing a summary of the note. "Maybe you should call her."

Toni's reply was cut off by a soft knocking on the door. Both girls locked stares momentarily before Julie moved to open the door as far as the safety chain could allow.

"Girlfriend," called Julie after a moment. "You have a visitor."

Toni instinctively knew before she entered the front room that she was about to be face to face with the woman who had all but destroyed her life.

Maggie Luke wasn't a bouffant blonde anymore. Her hair was short and an evenly dyed auburn. Her eyes weren't hard as Toni remembered them in her picture. They were nervous. They were the eyes of a woman no less than fifty years old.

The nervous flicker in her eyes was the only clue that she was not a statue. She stood so still and straight. Toni walked to the middle of the room and stopped, an odd feeling of sadness replacing her bitterness.

"Toni?" The older woman's chin twitched slightly as she offered her hand.

Toni nodded and shook hands quickly, uncomfortable with touching her.

"I'm Maggie Luke. I'd like to talk to you."

Toni gave her a searching glance before motioning her to follow her into the kitchen. Seating themselves across the tiny table from each other, a terrifying thought suddenly struck Toni. "Is Judd...all right?"

The older woman locked her eyes with Toni's. "No, Judd is *not* all right. That's why I'm here."

A sickening thud bounced in Toni's stomach. "Wh...what happened?"

A frown creased the woman's mouth. "You happened, Toni."

Toni sat rigidly speechless, waiting for a verbal attack. Instead, she watched the woman's face soften.

"Toni, I don't know what happened between you and my son. I didn't know what else to do but come here and...interfere."

Toni jerked bolt upright. "Your son? Your son?" She repeated, horrified, her dilated eyes registering an equally surprised set across the table.

"Why, yes. Judd is my son. I thought you knew that."

Toni dropped her face into her cupped hands, her elbows supporting the weight against the table top. She shook her head slowly. "No. I didn't know. I thought...Oh God in Heaven!"

"But Judd said that he told you."

Toni raised her ashen face. "He told me you were Mrs. Luke. I assumed he meant you were his..."

"Wife?" Maggie laughed with a childlike delight. "Well, make this old lady's day!"

Her laughter was kind, her eyes soft. The woman's laughter faded, her eyes genuinely seeking communication. "You are my daughter-in-law. And every bit as pretty as Judd claimed.

I'm not going to beat around the bush, but get right to the reason I'm here. "Do you love my son?"

"Yes," popped out before Toni was even consciously aware she'd said it.

"Well, there's no room to doubt that. So why did you leave him so abruptly then?"

The woman's straight to the point manner reminded Toni of Cowboy. A fresh surge of pain welled inside her and she strained to keep her emotions under control. "I saw you and Judd together at the house. I overheard...I saw you in his arms...Oh," Toni grabbed her stomach as nausea rose up. "I've made such a fool of myself." Her thoughts ran amuck, suddenly remembering out loud, "He was hurting...angry...yearning for someone...someone he lost. I thought..." She stopped when she saw a tear trickle down Maggie's cheek.

After a moment, the woman gathered control. She whispered, "Let me explain some things, honey." She hesitated as though the words forming in her mind were painful. "I'm not Judd's natural mother. Amy Luke died of cancer when Judd was only three years old. I married his father before Judd's fourth birthday. He was very attached to his mother. She remained at home during her illness and spent every moment with him. It was hard on him when she died. Of course he didn't understand and cried for his mother for months. Finally, I won him over and he clung to my side."

Maggie stared at the floor and Toni wondered if she were aware of the stream dripping from her cheeks. She continued after a moment. "I discovered too late that Judd's father was a tyrant toward women. He slapped me around a lot and I soon stopped loving him. I stayed with him because of Judd. That child needed me desperately. One evening, Jake came home from one of his many out of town trips and walked in on me and one of our ranch hands."

Toni felt herself sway and held to the table edge.

"I fled from the ranch that night. Jake would have killed me. I wasn't in love with the young cowboy. He offered to hold me and I needed that so bad." She shook her head and brushed the air with the back of her hand. "But never mind that. The issue here is Judd. He was sixteen years old at the time. He refused to see me after...after...well, I'm sure he never opened my letters. He believed I deserted him the same as he thought Amy did. I loved that boy as though he were my own blood."

Toni felt tears welling and her throat tightened. She finally knew the reason for Cowboy's insecurity about her love for him. And now..."Oh," she moaned as her hands came up to cover her face. She had walked out on her precious Cowboy when the worst pain he had was the fear of that very thing.

"Oh, Maggie," she moaned, her words coming out on a choked sob. "What have I done to him? I didn't know."

Maggie swiped at her eyes with the backs of her hands, straightened and reached across the table to move Toni's trembling hands from her face. This time the woman's touch was not offensive, but warm. "Well, that's right, you didn't know. And I'm going to tell you what Sky Cooper finally convinced me of. What's done is done. It can't be erased. But what you do from this moment on will mean the most."

For a moment, the two women took an intimate stock of each other, an immediate bond forming between them as they were drawn together by their love for one man.

Maggie broke the silence. "What about you and Judd?"

Toni felt her stomach churn. "I'm afraid I may have hurt him too deeply. He's fragile."

"Nonsense. Sensitive, yes, but not fragile. What I'm asking you, Toni, is do you love my son and your husband enough to go back home and fight for him?"

The question hung in the air between them until Toni's mind absorbed the implication of her words. Fight for him? "Then...you already know that he doesn't want me back, don't you?" she asked fearfully.

Maggie didn't look away nor try to smooth the truth. "Judd thinks he's through with you. He's angry. Bitter. That's not the question." Her eyes studied Toni's intently, waiting.

"Yes," Toni answered softly.

"Then go home to your husband and love him with all you've got." The older woman gave Toni a calm confident feeling. A renewed strength ebbed into her insides and a longing to rush back to her beloved Cowboy.

Toni stared solemnly at her hands folded on the table. Questions poured through her mind.

"What's wrong, honey. Talk to me."

"What contract were you talking about...the morning you and..."

Maggie held up a hand. "The Double OO Ranch, Toni, was mine. I was heir to it. After I married Judd's father...he badgered me to put his name on the title deed along with mine, but I never would consent. I think I always knew our marriage couldn't last. When I left the ranch to escape Jake's wrath and abuse. I never wanted to go back there. I was very ill, emotionally, for a long time. I wanted Judd to have the ranch and I drew up a contract stating that upon his wedding day, the Double OO would automatically become my wedding gift to him. Jake knew about the contract and I assumed he had told Judd. When Sky told me Judd had married so suddenly, I assumed it was so he could take over ownership of the ranch." She sighed heavily. "But that's the problem with most of this mess. We want to assume too much."

Toni moaned and closed her eyes. How could she have let him down so horribly? Pangs of guilt washed her again.

Maggie grabbed her arm and squeezed to snap her out of her self-condemnation. "Let it go, darlin. Judd needs your strength now like never before."

Toni sighed. "I don't think I've ever felt so weak and incapable in my life."

Maggie wanted to smile, but kept her face without expression. "I'm sure that will pass. Judd told me enough about you that I know you'll reel in that grit he's so fond of."

Toni's head jerked up, ears perked, "What do you mean?"

"Judd talked more about the strength his wife gave him than anything else. He seemed worried that he was taking so much from you and failing at giving anything back. Grit, he called it."

Toni's eyes filled. "He said that?"

"Yes, and..."

Toni caught the pained grimace that almost shook the woman's body before she continued.

"Life throws its punches. Some hit too hard and he has spent years trying to fight off the effects. It's made him hard."

"Or scared," Toni stated.

A mutual understanding leaped between them as they locked glances.

Maggie nodded her head slowly in agreement. Her voice came in a soft whisper, "I prayed to God that He would help my son. I know He sent you. You have wisdom beyond your years. Go to him, honey, and hold on to him and never let go."

Those familiar words were all Toni needed. Jumping up from her chair, she stepped over beside her new mentor and wrapped exhausted, but happy arms around the woman's neck.

***

CHAPTER TEN

Judd wasn't around when Toni entered the ranch house. She had arrived this time the same way as before.

She hadn't spoken to him since she'd left, deciding it would be better to just show up. At least he wouldn't have a chance to change the door locks.

The house was dark and surprisingly not so messy. In fact, it didn't look like he had spent any time here. A cold loneliness settled over her, like someone had died.

Suddenly, a little sick at her stomach, she felt restless and out of place. She had so much to make up for and blew it off as a guilt trip. It would be hard enough looking Cowboy in the eye. No sense compounding it with self-abasement. He'd probably do it for her anyway.

Toni woke the next morning with a start, the sharp sunlight blinding her. She got up and quietly peeked into the master bedroom knowing before she looked that it would be empty. The silence was deafening and loneliness sapped her confidence, sinking the pit of her stomach. The next minute she had her face hanging over the potty bowl, sick clear to her toes. Weakness flooded her. She sank to the floor and leaned her head against the bathtub, tears burning her cheeks.

She heard a truck drive up and the back door slam hard, but was too sick to care if the house fell in on her. She raised her head, swooned and threw up again, not believing for a minute she would live out the day.

The jangle of spurs sang in her ears. "What the..." Judd thundered behind her head. She didn't bother to try to look at him.

He swore softly jangling his spurs around the room, banged the closet door and ran water. She felt a hand cradle the back of her head as a cool wet cloth bathed her face.

"Can you get up?" The tenderness in his voice brought a fresh well in her throat.

She was afraid to move again, but before she could answer, taut muscled arms slid beneath her legs and around her back and lifted her slowly and gently. The cool sheets seemed to relieve her misery somewhat, but the fact that Cowboy carried her so tenderly to his, *their*, bed made her weepy again. He left and came back with a fresh wet cloth, folded it to a thin strip and draped it across her forehead.

It was then Toni actually looked him in the face. Stunned, she felt her heart break apart at the sight of him. He wasn't just work dirty, but looked like he hadn't eaten, shaved nor slept in days. His hair was long, his face pallid. But the degradation of heart she saw in his listless eyes was unbearable.

Judd stood there for a few seconds, just looking at her. "Will you be all right?" he spoke quietly.

"I was just wondering the same about you," she whispered, wishing he would lie down beside her.

"How long have you been here?" He ignored her concern for him.

"Since last evening."

"When are you leaving?" His tone was dead.

Toni's heart rhythm accelerated. "I'm not leaving, Cowboy." She could almost see a mask being drawn down his face. Vacant, yet mocking. An impenetrable look.

He left. She did not see him the remainder of that day nor did he come back that night.

After two days, she knew it was going to be up to her to force a confrontation. Judd was deliberately staying away. Testing her, maybe. Or hoping she'd give up and leave.

The matter was settled in her mind before Maggie ever left Julie's apartment that night. Toni wished she had her mother-in-law to talk to now. She had instilled a strength into Toni with her revelations of Cowboy's boyhood. She felt as though she were on a rescue mission. Given a little time and lots of TLC, her Cowboy would come back. She was confident.

From the looks of him a couple days ago, she figured he was camping out in his tent.

Toni finished eating and carried the dishes from the table to the sink. Her mind began creating a plan. After washing up, she checked the time and calculated there was plenty of daylight left.

The flatbed truck was gone but the big gelding she'd rode several times was loose in the arena.

A short while later, she cinched the saddle girth tight, mounted and set off through the pasture and mountain cedars. The horse knew exactly where he was going. Toni let the big bay have his head down the creek bank. The crossing was steep, but she trusted her surefooted friend who whinnied loudly, declaring their presence.

Toni let her legs dangle outside the saddle stirrups, her face tilted to catch the fullness of a north breeze. It dawned on her that the season had changed...She had already discovered that wind was a constant in Wyoming. Night and day there was some kind of wind blowing.

Wintertime in the high country. The thought was exhilarating. She was back in her element. That had to be the reason for the sweetness she felt in her soul. This was home. This is where she belonged. Thank you, God, she offered.

Following a clear cut trail through the now steep timber, she came presently to the edge of the valley where cattle were scattered and grazing. There were no horses or hands in sight. Maybe they were working in another area. Her heart sank. Maybe Cowboy wasn't staying in the tent after all.

She rode downward nearly to the clearing to view the well-defined trail leading back up to the tent. A falling dusk and chilly wind was all there was. And silence. Even the cattle were quiet.

Suddenly the gelding stiffened, ears alert. He heard it before Toni did, an unmistakable crunch of pine needles pressing into the ground behind her.

The horse started, but Toni picked up on the reins. "Easy", she whispered and patted his taut neck. The sound came again and Toni's stomach flipped over. Fear clutched at her throat and a split second before she would have moved out fully into the clearing and away from the shadowy timber, a large hand grabbed hers along with the reins.

"Whoa, bay." A low throaty growl came from the blurry figure that quickly took advantage of the empty stirrup and came up behind the saddle to straddle the horse's rump.

Cowboy's unmistakable snarl grated into her ear as the bay instantly regarded his new master's command to walk forward.

Toni fought hard to stop her heart from flying up her throat. If she could have reached around herself, she would have slapped him right back off for scaring her out of her wits.

Minutes later, he turned the gelding into the corral with another horse. He pulled the saddle and draped it over the top rail and latched the gate.

He appeared to have forgotten she was there until he stepped inside the tent and threw a blue jean jacket back out at her. He disappeared inside again and presently a lantern light glowed from the interior.

"It's warmer in here," he stated matter-of-factly. Toni thought he sounded too controlled.

She opened the flap and froze at the hollow bitterness in his face. "Come in at your own risk." The words warned like the crack of a whip.

"I'll take my chances," she slung back and stepped inside.

She stared at him, taking her first good look since she returned. He looks older, she thought. Cutting. Hurt. Her heart raced.

She walked to where he sat on the thick quilted pallet and squatted beside him. She took his unresponsive hand into hers and squeezed as though to stir some life back into him.

"Cowboy, I'm so sorry, I..."

He jerked his hand away. "Let it go, Toni."

She shook her head slowly, registering the depth of contempt in his voice. "I can't let it go. And I'm not leaving." She shivered involuntarily. It was very dark now and the cold was penetrating.

His deadpan expression fixed itself on her face. He stood up, grasped her arm and brought her up with him. His breath became ragged and heavy suddenly, a mixture of rage and desire building behind gray pools.

Toni took a step backward, thoughts of fleeing into the cold darkness momentarily sounded better than contending with the fire aimed at her.

Silence seemed to stretch into eternity. Toni saw the passion that was clearly whipping his pride. A full blown war raged inside him.

Five seconds more and Toni would have thrown herself into him, begging for her Cowboy's forgiveness.

But the words he ground between barely moving lips, shattered the violent longing that had captured the space between them.

"Get out of here, Toni. Now!"

It took a few seconds to absorb the impact. "I'm not leaving." She stood her ground, defying the barrage of warning in his voice.

Iron hard fingers clasped her chin and forced her face upward. "Do you have to learn everything the hard way?" he grated. Then his mouth crashed heavily on hers.

Toni's senses raged with desire and she returned the fierceness of his kiss, not discerning her husband's total lack of control.

He pushed her back a step and before she realized what he was doing, her jeans were unfastened and yanked down over her slender hips. The savagery with which he slammed her body down to the blankets brought a cry of alarm from deep in her throat. Her shirt buttons flew in every direction and with one jerk, he tore it partially off her shoulders.

"No," she moaned. "No."

His concrete length came down on top of her and made her fully aware that she was completely exposed down to her knees and Judd's shirt was gone.

A thick moan rose up from his depths as he pulled her tighter into him, roughly pressing her breasts. A hot searing pain rolled through her upper body. She tried to muffle the scream that sprang from her throat but, too late.

Judd jerked up off of her, the painful cry snapping his senses to attention. "What the...," he spit, trying to gain control over the delirious desire that shook him to the core of his being.

Toni felt his hand touch the side of her face. He cursed again when he found her cheek wet with tears.

"I ought to be horsewhipped," he muttered between his teeth. He pulled her up to sit beside him. "What did I do? Where are you hurt?"

She couldn't speak and when his hand came up and touched a swollen breast, she flinched and sharply sucked in her breath.

"Ouch. They hurt. Please don't touch me there." She was visibly shaken by the attack.

He pulled back. "What do you mean, they hurt? I mean, why?" He looked bewildered.

Toni closed her eyes almost willing her brain not to think what she already knew. Instinctively her hand went to her stomach, her gaze following it.

Judd's eyes widened with shock before he jumped to his feet and grabbed a long sleeved heavy denim work shirt from a box and dropped it in her lap. "Put this on."

Spinning, he pulled a Coleman stove to the center of the tent, pumped it up and began warming the small space. He seemed to be trying to fill time.

Toni replaced her torn clothing with the big shirt and pulled her jeans back in place.

Judd kept his back to her. She knew he was waging a battle within himself, discovering that she was pregnant. But she didn't expect the clench lipped fury that suddenly whirled across the small space of the tent at her.

"Why didn't you tell me?" His lips quivered with anger.

"I...I wasn't sure. Not until now." Toni's insides knotted. Was he angry that she carried his child?

"Is that why you came back? Because you suspected you might be left to raise a baby by yourself?"

"No, Cowboy, no. I came home because I found out that Maggie was your mama. And that she..."

"My mama!" he cut her off sharply. "Who did you think she was?"

Toni swallowed hard. "I saw the two of you at the house together. At your house."

She watched the anger in his face change from surprise to...was it disappointment?

"You were in my house?" Confusion spread across his face. "But...how did you...?"

She licked her lips and looked away, then back up at his waiting stare. "I rode up on the place the day of my accident. I had no idea it belonged to you. I meant to ask you about it, but...I forgot about it."

His expression was indefinable as he waited for her to continue.

"I...I knew Maggie was coming to the ranch to see you that morning. I intercepted a phone call to verify her visit. I knew you left me in the tent to go see her.

"How did you know where to come to?" His voice thankfully softened.

"Doyle told me."

"Doyle?"

"He stopped me before I could drive out. He wanted me to take you some paperwork, um, some measurements for something. He made sure I remembered the directions to your house, the easy way around. In case I'd forgotten. So I drove there and went in."

In the ensuing silence, they stared at each other. Toni, trying to read a forgiving expression, but he was back to stone faced.

"I'm sorry that...you didn't get Doyle's paper. I'm not sure where it is now."

"I got it. Found it on the floor in the foyer." He spoke as though it was of no importance. He seemed to be reaching back in his mind to make sense of something. "I thought Doyle had come by. But you were there." He paused in reflection. "You must have seen me comforting her. Five minutes of an emotional moment between me and my mother."

"I thought, oh heavens, I thought she was...your ex-wife."

Surprise lit his face. "Where did you get that idea? I told you..."

"You only told me she was Mrs. Luke. I couldn't read your mind to know the rest."

"It doesn't seem you can read a man's heart either, not even when he takes it out and lays it bare before the woman who has filled it up."

The hurt in his eyes pierced her like a dagger through the heart. She stood and closed the gap between them, throwing her arms around his stiffened middle. She had to make him know she loved him more than her own life. He *was* her life.

"Cowboy," she whispered against his chest, tightening her grip.

Hard fingers clasped her upper arms and pushed her back until her grasp broke and she stood, rejected by the one man on the planet who could destroy her, heart and soul.

Cold, he glared down at her. "There's one thing you managed to get right, Mrs. Luke. You *won't* be leaving me. Not with my baby in your belly."

A long tense moment lapsed in which neither spoke. She almost hated him for a moment. Then nothing. After a moment, something indefinable, a calmness flowed through her veins. She wasn't sure what it was that was so quiet, reserved in even the air around her. She recalled this same feel in the air around her the first day she had stepped up on the ranch house porch.

Then it hit her. Like a revelation truth that left her momentarily stunned. The Double OO Ranch was home. She was home, despite the circumstances. She knew all the way to the bottom of herself that this is where she belonged, where God had meant for her to be. She had a family again. Cowboy and Maggie and Cowboy's baby. And time. Time was her ace.

From the angry distrust aimed at her she knew the confidence in her heart at that moment would have to carry her through.

Judd broke the silence. "When will you have the baby?"

She hadn't had time to think about it, but calculated quickly. "April or May, I figure."

"You'd better see a doctor."

"Yes." She answered absently, then, "What do you want me to do, Cowboy?"

"About what?" he shot stonily.

She needed to hear him say that he wanted her to stay with him. To make a home and be a family. I want everything to be simple, she thought, as she turned her face up to look at him in the yellow lantern light.

"Us." she whispered calmly.

His eyes bore through hers, a jaw muscle exerting itself. "Let me clue you in. Marriage doesn't mean that much. Commitment is just a word. Whatever we had here, it's over."

Toni's insides grabbed painfully. "No, Judd. Maybe we both had better slide off our self-centered mounts and think about this baby we made."

Anger rushed color to Judd's face. "We!" he exploded. He took hold of her then and she could see his fight to restrain himself from shaking her as his fingers dug cruelly into her slight upper arms. "Do you have any idea how crazy I was after you left? Not one single word. You just disappeared and never called. For days I sat by that phone until Julie called and told me where you were."

"Julie!"

He laughed, mocking her. "Yeah, Julie. You can always count on a woman's betrayal."

She struggled to let that one go by..."Did you send Maggie?"

"Maggie. Where?

"Nothing," she mumbled, hoping he would let it go.

"What has my mother got to do with this?" he grated at her.

"Judd, I don't know...She...nothing."

"Answer my question," he said flatly, his eyes deadpan.

She sighed in defeat. "She came to see me in Dallas. That's when I found out who she was. She was worried about you, Cowboy."

"She talked you into coming back." He said it as though he was thinking out loud. "You had no intention of coming home, did you?" His voice was painfully sober.

Toni's restraint broke then. "That's the spirit, Cowboy. Fill up a beer can. Slam the door on everyone who cares about you. And by all means, don't forgive anybody. I mean, if the people in your life can't be perfect for you...perfect parents and a perfect wife and have no emotional baggage to deal with of their very own, well just stomp 'em under your boots and walk on. Be a tough man like your daddy!"

The look he gave her went from surprise to confusion, like he'd just been slapped hard across the face. When the shock broke, his voice boomed like a cannon, his eyes supplying the fire. "What did you say?"

The part about his daddy had slipped out unintentionally, and the blackness in his face brought a very intentional *Jesus help me* cry from her heart. "I'm sorry. I...shouldn't have said..."

The apology cut short as she jerked her head sideways and jutted out an elbow to shield her face from his hand that was raised high in the air.

"Don't! Please don't," Her fearful shriek came out in a whisper.

He lowered his arm slowly and Toni watched the blood drain from his face. His shock was aimed at his own still partially raised hand.

"What am I doing?" He murmured under his breath, but Toni heard.

Even at this moment, she still felt a yearning inside her to reach out to this tortured man who had carried her heart around for so long. Only God knew why. Then a thought spoke in her head. It was God's love that she carried inside of her that was reaching out to comfort Cowboy, even as he very nearly committed this act of abuse. But she didn't move.

Judd raked a hand through his long dirty hair that had been flattened by his hat. Toni could see him visibly shaking and swallowing again and again to wash the threatening lump down. Keeping his eyes diverted from her, he spoke so quietly. "The truck is behind the tent. I'll drive you home."

Silence cloaked the pair in the bare moonlight, as they sat in the truck now parked behind the ranch house. Neither made a sound. There was only darkness and the steady ticking of the truck radiator as it cooled.

"You can't hide forever, Cowboy. Sooner or later you'll have to face whatever is eating you up."

He let out a long slow breath and turned behind the steering wheel to face his wife in the cold darkness. "Don't try to play the savior for me, Toni. I came close to hurting you tonight."

She met his gaze. He sounded whipped. The anger was gone, replaced with weariness in the outline of his face. How badly she wanted to wrap him up in her arms and love all the pain from those haunted blue eyes. She wanted her playful, laughing Cowboy back.

From who knew where, a sudden gleeful lightheartedness waved it's wand over her head and she took a giddy stab at him. "Did you really miss me after I left, Cowboy?"

His eyes widened on her, but she pushed on.

"Or was it my sunny side up eggs draped over a stack of flapjacks?"

An incredulous look crossed his face. "You think this is a big joke, don't you?"

"I think you need to lighten up, that's what I think. So, what's your answer?" A ridiculous exuberance urged her on.

"Answer to what?"

"Was it me you missed or the flapjacks?" She shot him a sideways glance, hoping to see that the lines in his face had softened.

He turned his head to look toward the house. Without answering her, Judd whisked open the truck door, stepped out and held it open for her. His expression was unreadable.

Once inside the house, he disappeared into the bathroom and within seconds, Toni heard the shower running. It crossed her mind to strip down and join him, but decided one more rejection today was too many. Instead she changed to a cotton night shirt and curled up on the guest room bed.

Through the bedroom wall, she listened to the steady spray of water. It took all of Toni's strength not to break down. She breathed deep for control, but her heart tightened. Had she lost his heart? Had she hurt him too deeply by walking out the way she did? Love couldn't die away because of one foolish mistake, could it? One really bad mistake. Tears trickled from the corners of her closed eyelids. "Jesus," she whispered. "Jesus."

Judd had reached into the shower and turned on the cold water spray to help drown out the raging turmoil he feared might fly up his throat. He backed against the bathroom door; put his head back and shut his eyes.

His entire body trembled; every nerve seemed to be stretching past the limit. One arm pressed across his middle as he bent over, suddenly nauseous. Oh God! What had he just done? He swallowed and swallowed, staring at the tiled floor only a couple of feet from his face. The shower ran full blast, the noise only amplifying the lonely darkness invading his guts, heavy and oppressive. It was all he could do not to puke.

He had nearly raped his wife. He had raised his hand to hit her like he had watched his daddy hit his mom so many times. And he'd hated him for that. He'd hated his mom for whoring around with some hired hand who lived in the bunk house. He had hated her for running away, even though he understood why. And here he was imitating that very behavior. His hatred of it had all but eaten him alive and it was about to cost him the most precious gift he'd ever had. *His wife. His baby.* God, they deserved better than this.

All he wanted to do was hold and protect Toni. The love she carried around in her little finger was more than he deserved, and yet she'd given him all she had. She made him happier than he'd ever known was possible. He couldn't bear the thought of not having her. More than that, he couldn't stomach the idea of hurting her again.

"Oh, Jesus," he moaned into the air. "Help me."

He dropped to his knees and obliviously jerked his hat off of his head, tossing the dusty bent up straw across the floor. His urge was to look up, to search for God, to beg Him for help. But he couldn't raise his head nor his eyes. Judd had tossed up a prayer now and again throughout his life, but this time was different. Every cell in his body, his heart, his will, his reason all seemed to be reaching upward, but having to strain against the gravity that held his flesh and bone. This time, reaching out to God was a struggle, but he *would not, could not* turn loose.

After a few soul wrenching moments, he heard himself whispering, face almost touching the floor, "Forgive me. Forgive me." Long pent up tears came. He let them come freely until he was spent.

Toni jumped suddenly, then realized she'd been asleep. She felt like she had slept quite a while. When her eyes adjusted, the room was softly bathed in lamplight.

Standing there leaning against the door frame was her Cowboy, a bath towel wrapped around his middle. He wasn't smiling, but a light shown in his eyes she had never seen before, almost creating a transformation in his whole being.

What Cowboy felt at this moment couldn't seem to go into a rational sounding thought. He had put his wife and unborn baby under the gun of physical abuse. Emotional torment. And not until a few moments ago, did he even begin to see how vile, evil that was. Something indefinable for him had just happened in that bathroom.

That was his wife laying there. But more than that, he felt a brand new connection to her, as though she was as much a part of his body as he was. Her need for love and happiness, for fullness of life on this earth was suddenly the most important thing in the world to him.

There was almost a desperation to defend this oneness he was feeling with Toni. To defend it even from himself, from his own failures as a man, a husband.

Could he love her any more than this? Somehow he knew there was more. Way more. He just didn't understand it yet.

Toni didn't have to wonder at the sudden visible change she saw on her husband's face. She had seen it before at the cowboy church meetings she used to attend with Uncle John. She had even experienced it herself. In her intuitive knower, Toni recognized that her husband had visited with God.

She looked at him, deep and searching and he looked back at his wife for a long time. The semi-darkness didn't fully conceal the puffiness under his eyes. This macho Wyoming cowboy had broken.

With his eyes still locked on hers, he walked toward her slowly. Etched across his face was a sweet, gentle and so slight smile, his eyes sparkling with blue fire and gazing into her now wet, shimmering pools.

He stopped beside the bed and let the towel drop to the floor, his eyes never leaving hers. "I came to answer your question." The deep intensity of his voice enflamed her senses.

Judd stretched out beside her. He gathered her up in his arms and held her like a fragile, priceless jewel. He held her long into the night, at times caressing her face, her hair and kissing her lips as gentle as he would kiss a baby.

Once, Toni felt his body shake and heard him weeping into her hair. She hardly moved at all, could barely breath inside of this precious, almost holy experience they were sharing together. The love expressed between them was so pure and undiluted, it made Toni cry.

His hand brushed the tears from her cheeks, and he kissed the salty wetness that dripped on her lips. "I know," he choked, still weepy. "I know."

They lay wrapped together for a long time in a sweet dreamlike peace. Neither one slept, but savored every second as though their lives together were ending rather than just beginning.

For days afterward, Toni felt different inside. Older maybe. She felt like she no longer needed to be soothed and coddled. It seemed more of an added wonderful pleasure to be held in Cowboy's strong, protective and loving arms, but a greater need, a higher priority for her being here took precedence. Her entire being, spirit, body and soul now needed desperately to soothe, to coddle, to pour her love into her husband. And no matter how long it took or how many set-backs would come, she had surrendered herself up to see it through.

This is what she had been raised up to do...to love God and to love Cowboy.

One month later, Toni saw Cowboy's big log home looming before her, only it was a dusky evening and the front yard and wrap around porch was softly lighted. Eight foot high outdoor lamps on ornate wrought iron bases lined a long cedar chip walkway to the slate steps. An archway stood several feet from the steps, covered with daisies sprinkled amidst every kind of color of wild flower, sprigs and thistles she'd ever seen, and some she hadn't...a perfect match to the bride's bouquet she held in her hands.

Toni sat on the quilt padded seat of a small, creaky wagon between her best friend, Julie and Doyle Williamson. She couldn't help but notice what a handsome man Doyle was all dressed up in new leather chaps that buckled over his jeans and a white pearl snap western shirt. His straw Stetson was new too. He didn't seem at all uncomfortable, but held his gaze straight ahead as he expertly handled Cook's two black and white speckled mules that pulled the small wagon.

Cowboy had forbid her to go near this house until he gave permission. He wanted them to re-new their vows first. Maggie had *helped* her shop for a wedding dress in Jackson, Cowboy's idea, two weeks earlier and that was all the information she could pry out of the woman. Only that Judd was planning a *little outing* for them to renew their vows properly. Toni decided to keep quiet and let them have their fun until Judd had instructed Maggie to deck her out in long, fancy and white with all the spangles and bangles. A beautiful pure white string of pearls was left on her dressing table from Cowboy.

Then when Julie showed up at the ranch house door about two hours before she was to meet Judd for their *little outing*, and dressed in an elaborate long beige evening gown and carrying a bridal bouquet for the bride, the jig was up. She didn't know what the jig was. But it was definitely up.

And here she was, being delivered by a mule drawn wagon to what appeared to be an old fashioned, charmingly decorated lawn party...wedding. Hers and Cowboys. She felt a little nervous, but excited, now that she was viewing the details of her *little outing*, a surprise planned for her by her adorable husband. Julie was momentarily speechless as the wagon rolled to a stop in front of the log house she had secretly heard about from Maggie just a few days ago. She squeezed Toni's hand in an attempt to quell her own excitement that wanted to squeal out of her open mouth.

Toni's eyes scanned the scene when the wagon came to a stop. "Oh my gosh." Her hand came up and covered her opened mouth three times before she could get it shut. Happy tears burned her eyes while Doyle, planning ahead, handed her a fresh Kleenex without looking over at her.

Everyone watched, knowing this had all been kept secret from her. There were faces she didn't know, but figured they were business friends of Judd's, another life's work he hadn't mentioned until a month ago.

Ranching was his passion...the very life that flowed in his veins. Real estate was his main living. A very good living, at that. She could certainly get used to all the new *tidbits* she was learning about this saddle-bum husband of hers.

Tables covered in yellow gingham held paper plates, drinks and gifts. A three-tier wedding cake with a bride and groom astraddle a rearing white horse on the top layer adorned one table alone. Hay bales for seating encircled the entire area. Cook's chuck wagon was set up and adorned with lighted lanterns and large bunches of wild flowers tied with strips of yellow gingham lay amid bowls and platters of all the chuck wagon fixins imaginable.

On the opposite side of the yard, hay bales were lined up like rows of benches with a wide open center aisle, the flower entwined archway waiting at the far end. Toni noticed that most of the guests, all looking her way and applauding, wore a more casual attire of boots and jeans.

And Maggie. There she stood just to the side of the archway. Her long pale yellow gown fit in more with the wedding party's glitzy-wear. She was grinning ear to ear and swiping at tears as the two women's eyes met.

Just then a parade of young men in cowboy hats approached the wagon. "Oh." Toni giggled in pure delight. The Double OO cowboys. Her own band of big brothers. Once when she had been injured and cold, they had all taken off their shirts to keep her warm. Now they were all dressed fit to kill, circling her wagon in greeting, pink cheeked and grinning. She didn't think her heart could take on anymore joy.

"Allow me, gentlemen." Les elbowed his way through the group. He reached up and caught Julie around her small waist and helped her to the ground. Toni grinned as she caught the big deal that Les was making out of setting her maid of honor softly and gently on her feet, taking his time to help smooth out her dress, before escorting her down the pathway to her honored spot.

As Toni gathered up her skirts and long train, it was Doyle who reached to help her from the wagon.

The wedding march began and Toni noticed Sky standing across from Julie and occupying the best man's place of honor. Not in a year's time could she have arranged her own wedding any more perfect.

Doyle offered Toni his arm.

"Thank you. Are you doing me the great honor of giving me away?"

"Yes, ma'am. It's my pleasure to do it." His face flushed a little.

C.J., better known as Cook, stepped up and offered his arm on her opposite side. "I'd be pleased to be givin' you away too, Mrs. Luke." Toni grasped his arm feeling like pure royalty and not all surprised at the huge lump that formed in her throat.

"Me, too." It was Les.

Peggy Patrick

"I'll be walking with you too," another voice came from behind her.

Toni swallowed hard and felt Doyle reach up to squeeze her hand that held his arm. It was the cowboys...her rescuers and new family that flanked her on both sides. They all wore new leather chaps over their jeans and white western shirts with a wild flower peeping out of the pockets. "You guys are going to make me cry."

A.J. picked up the train of her gown and quipped, "Head'em up and move'em out before we have to wade a creek to get there."

They all stifled laughter as an amplifier blasting the wedding march moved the bride and her entourage down the path where Judd now stood beneath the archway. His eyes locked on Toni's and the air space between them filled up with a lover's Fourth of July style sparkle that momentarily blinded them from all but each other. He wore a white tux that blended with his bride's formal gown. *Something old, something new*, she thought, as she mentally contrasted the elaborately dressed bride and groom with the more rustic cowboy décor around the yard. How original. Perfect. Toni knew her dress was what Cowboy wanted to see her in. And if she never saw her man dressed in more than worn out boots, jeans and work shirt again, she would savor this moment of the two of them, dressed to the wedding day nines for each other, for the rest of her life. He was truly God's gift to her standing there waiting for her arrival.

SURRENDERED

Toni was hardly aware of anyone else as she walked toward her husband. Her stomach was already protruding with the presence of its little passenger, but nothing could have pleased the parents more...or the wedding party and guests. Judd thanked the guys as they delivered her safe and sound into his hand. Before turning to the minister for the traditional ceremony, Judd turned to Toni and held both of her hands in his.

"Toni," he began, pausing to regroup his emotions. "You've been my wife for several months now. You've said more than once that you didn't care about having a wedding with all the trappings involved. But, you deserve a wedding day to remember. Our wedding day. This house was in the process of being finished when you came to the ranch. I chose to keep it a secret until it was complete because I wanted it to be a special gift, a surprise for you. My mom worked a few dozen miracles during this past month to help me accomplish this." He glanced at Maggie who was openly weeping now. "Thanks, Mom." He pulled Toni closer in to him. "This is where you live now. This is our home. And this is our wedding day to remember for the rest of our lives." He paused a moment, and swallowed at the lump forming in his throat, but never took his eyes from hers. "There's one more thing. I want to say this to you before...before God and everybody here." After another pause, he continued. "I want to thank you for being so tolerant of my failures as a man these past months. My failure as a husband. I love you so much. But feeling it and doing it right...well...I'm learning. Thank you for allowing me time to learn to get it right."

She could barely see his face through the shimmering haze of tears. She had never once seen him as a failure. Somehow she knew his public confession he'd just made to her was far more difficult for him than he made it appear, but it was a moment of healing for both of them. Pride had just been dealt a finishing blow inside his tough cowboy interior. For her, a total forgiveness and release of lingering hurt that she had shoved down in her depths.

Toni was radiant and teary-eyed. And now, staring into the depths of her husband's eyes, his spirit, she had to remind herself that for the intensity of the love she was viewing there, her heart swelling almost to bursting, he was flesh and blood man who needed her love desperately. He would give her his very breath because the God-love inside of him now had taught him how to truly love her. As she squeezed his hands tightly, she vowed to do her part and with all of her being.

"You've made me the happiest woman in the world, Cowboy." She patted her bulging middle. "I'm doubly blessed beyond my wildest dreams. Thank *you*, sweetheart."

They gazed at each other, both of their hearts glittering with love in their misty eyes.

They turned; fingers entwined, and faced the minister.

A few hours later, Cowboy swung his bride and baby-in-waiting up into his arms and carried them effortlessly across their new threshold. Toni was hoping for a tour of her new home, but Cowboy walked quickly down a long hallway to a closed set of massive pine double doors before setting her on her feet in front of them.

Judd caught his wife's face between his big leather-calloused hands. "I want you to know before I open these doors that no one, not even me, has slept in this room. There is nothing left that I haven't told you about, Toni. My life is an open book to you. It always will be. And this room is mine and yours alone...our private haven that no one can share." He leaned back and looked down at her tummy bump, squinting his eyes. "Well, except for Cowboy Pecos, there."

She laughed, "What if it's Annie Oakley?"

"We'll keep her." He grinned broadly. "I guess I better get used to sharing these, too." He bent and lightly kissed the swells of her growing breasts.

The most tender look Toni had ever seen on his face fixed itself on hers as he reached and pushed open the big doors.

Toni caught her breath at the sight before her. The master bedroom was sunken with four terra cotta ceramic tiled steps leading down onto the same richly tiled floor. Yellow lamplight set into the log walls spread a cozy warm glow around the entire room.

She slowly walked down the steps, barely breathing as her eyes moved over the huge king sized log bed covered in a turquoise blue and beige plaid quilted comforter. The matching bedside tables were massive with black lamps made with welded horseshoes and dark tan leather lampshades. She was stunned at the beauty and perfection of the décor. This room was like looking at a picture in Mountain Life Magazine.

A smaller set of double doors on the far side of the room were opened, drawing Toni to peek inside. Lamplight incased within log walls revealed a large hot tub and shower area enclosed by large rocks and foliage and a slab of rock with a trickling fall of water running over it.

She slapped her hands over her mouth in sheer excitement. "Cowboy, it's just like our honeymoon place in the creek!"

Judd stood in the doorway above the steps, watching her with a sheepish grin on his face that revealed just how proud he was feeling of himself. His heart was about to explode at the joy on her face. *God, help me to always be good to my wife.*

The only part of Toni's wedding attire she still wore was the dress. She turned around and locked wet sparkling eyes on her husband. Within a few seconds, she let the dress billow to the floor around her feet.

Without taking his eyes from hers, Cowboy stepped inside the room and pushed the doors closed behind him.

****

PREVIEW OF

BOOK TWO IN THE

SURRENDERED SERIES

Surrendered II Preview

Martha watched the crew ride back in and dismount. It was a little after 3AM. She had seen the truck and horse trailer lights leave the barn about an hour ago and return just minutes ahead of the riders.

Andy had been tucked in hours ago, but Martha sat up waiting for Jesse.

The storm had passed through just after midnight. Laura wouldn't answer her cabin phone and when Martha ran over to check on her, found she had never been there. She had checked the barn and even the teepees, thinking maybe she got caught out there in the storm.

When Jesse headed across the yard toward the house, she met him part way. When he noticed the worry lines etched so tightly around her eyes, he began filling her in, even before he reached her.

"Rebel Man's hurt. Cut up in barbed wire, but we got him home. Donny's calling Les now and…"

"Jesse," she broke in, swallowing a rising panic. "I can't find Laura."

His eyes rounded in disbelief. "What do you mean, you can't find her?"

"I sent her to her cabin before the storm hit. She wouldn't answer the phone during the storm and afterwards I walked around the place to check on the animals and things. I decided to peep inside her cabin to make sure she was all right. But it didn't look like she ever got there. Her bed was still made."

"Where's Andy?"

"Asleep here in the guest room."

Jesse turned almost a complete circle as if trying to decide which way to go first. "Maybe she ran into one of the other cabins...got caught in the rain."

"No, I looked in all of them. I even checked the teepees."

He raised his hat off of his head just enough to rake his hand through his hair, then settled it back on. If he had ever been this exhausted before, he couldn't remember it. The worry mixing with it wasn't helping.

He looked toward the barn where Donny and some of the hands were taking care of his injured horse. When his gaze went back to Martha, he was already moving toward the drive way. "I'll take the jeep and drive around. Martha, check those cabins again," he yelled as he jogged into the darkness.

She was across the road and almost running when it hit her. The honeymoon cabin. No. She'd never have gone there in a storm, in the dark, on foot. But she turned suddenly and ran after Jesse before he could drive away.

"The old line shack. Drive out that direction."

Jesse looked like Martha had run out there and thrown a bucket of cold water on him.

"Trust me on this, Jesse. It's the only place I haven't looked."

He drove away then, shaking his head at Martha. *Poor old woman. I hope that's not Alzheimer's disease starting in on her.*

Jesse drove to every cabin including Laura's. He looked inside her SUV that was parked in her driveway, then circled the perimeter of the ranch yard twice. His stomach muscles had tightened. This didn't make sense. He stopped the jeep in the driveway and let the engine idle a moment.

Lord Jesus, show me something here. I really need Your help.

He saw headlights turn into the ranch and recognized Les Kane's veterinary truck. Strangely he didn't feel overly alarmed about Laura, but decided he needed to get help to locate her. He started toward the barn when Martha stepped outside the back door of the house and jabbed her finger toward the back side of the barn toward the gate that led out toward the old line shack. He couldn't keep from rolling his eyes. *Good Lord! I'm going to have her head examined right after I get mind done!*

He shot through the gate and followed a muddy, but worn road in the direction of the old abandoned shack. Who had been driving a vehicle out here lately that would make a road so visible? And why was *he* driving on it now, besides humoring an old woman? After everything else that he'd seen since he got home this evening, *nothing* could surprise him. Not even his own idiocy.

He was, however, surprised at his calm demeanor as he slowly made his way through mud and slick grass. Wherever Laura was, he felt inside himself that she wasn't in any danger. Maybe he had embarrassed her or scared her and she was hiding out, even though that didn't sound like her. Come to think of it, he hadn't searched the barn. Nah. She wasn't the type to curl up in a horse stall or on a hay bale. Or was she? After what she had done to his ranch the past couple weeks, she could be Jack the freekin Ripper underneath that beautiful and deceptively innocent face!

But Lord Almighty, she actually thinks she's half owner of High Point. *That would be MY office,* he mocked her, remembering her saucy little remark.

Suddenly, he burst out laughing until he had to stop the jeep and lay his head on the steering wheel. He didn't want to laugh. Nightmares are not funny, but he couldn't stop. He laughed until he wiped tears away with the backs of his hands.

Laughter doeth good like a medicine.

Was that a scripture that just rose up in his mind?" "I don't *want* to laugh right now, thank YOU very much," he said aloud. Then he doubled over again until he was out of breath.

He sat for a few minutes after the laughter died away, surprised at how relaxed his body felt. Maybe God was trying to keep him from choking a woman to death tonight. And then again, maybe he'd just gone and lost his mind!

He shoved the floor shift in gear. The old shack was just around the corner. He'd turn around in front of it and go back to the yard and do a more thorough search.

He could barely make out the outline of the shack as he rounded the bend, but when his headlights shone on the front of the building, Jesse simultaneously hit his brake and stared, bug-eyed and open mouthed.

The front door was freshly painted red. An old weathered and broken piece of board with writing painted on it hung by a piece of baling wire in the upper middle section of that red door. Was that daisies circled around the sign? He squinted his eyes trying to read it. *Honeymoon Hideout.*

His eyes moved to the long wooden box sitting underneath the window and filled with various colored wildflowers, then to a brightly colored rug lying like a welcome mat on the porch floor.

What in the name of Uncle Sam Hill had happened here? For the first time since he got home, he felt completely unnerved. His stomach was queasy suddenly. He hadn't eaten a bite since breakfast and it was nearly breakfast again. He was beyond exhausted. He had laughed like a silly school girl a minute ago and now his whole body had frozen into a mannequin-like state at this ridiculous image of his dilapidated old line shack. Maybe his truck *had* rolled on top of him.